Beyond the Cracked Mirror

Beyond the Cracked MIRROR

To my family, thank you for your love, patience, and encouragement. This book is dedicated to you.

Synopsis

Beyond the Cracked Mirror

In the quaint, historic town of Hawthorne Heights, nothing is as it seems. The cobblestone streets and colonial-era buildings conceal a dark and sinister past, about to resurface with a chilling force. The town's fragile peace is shattered when Michael, a close friend of Ella Harper, vanishes without a trace.

As fear grips the tight-knit community, Ella and her friends—Liam Turner, Jade Morris, and Noah Bennett—are determined to uncover the truth behind his mysterious disappearance.

Their quest leads them to an abandoned mansion on the edge of town, rumored to be haunted and filled with eerie whispers and broken mirrors. Inside, they discover cryptic symbols and remnants of a buried history.

As they investigate further, they unearth a terrifying secret: Hawthorne Heights was founded by a cult that worshipped a malevolent entity known as "The Whisperer." This dark force demands a sacrifice every twenty years to maintain its sinister grip on the town.

With Michael's life at stake, the teens must race against time to reveal the cult's secrets and thwart the impending ritual. Noah's research at the town library unveils old diaries and documents that piece together the town's occult past. As the ritual's climax draws near, Ella and her friends must stay united to save Michael and prevent him from becoming the next victim in the cycle of sacrifices.

Chapter 1

The Disappearance

Ella Harper stood at the edge of Hawthorne Heights' town square, her gaze drifting over the cobblestone streets and the quaint shops that lined them. It was a picture-perfect summer day, with the sun casting a warm glow over the historic buildings and casting long shadows in the late afternoon.

But beneath the surface tranquility, Ella sensed an unease lingering in the air. It had been three days since Michael's disappearance, and the town was gripped by a palpable tension. Michael had been her friend since childhood, his easy smile and mischievous spirit a constant presence in her life. Now, his absence left an unsettling void.

Nearby, Liam Turner leaned against the base of the town's old fountain, flipping through a worn notebook with furrowed brows.

Liam, the newcomer to Hawthorne Heights, had quickly become entangled in the mystery surrounding Michael's vanishing. His logical mind sought patterns where others saw only shadows.

Jade Morris, on the other hand, paced nervously beside Ella, her dark eyes darting to every corner of the square as if expecting Michael to appear out of thin air. Jade was cautious by nature, her apprehension a stark contrast to Ella's determination to find answers.

Noah Bennett approached them, a stack of dusty books clutched against his chest. Noah, with his wire-rimmed glasses and perpetual curiosity, had spent countless hours in the town library digging for clues about Hawthorne Heights' hidden past. His latest findings promised to shed light on the dark undercurrents swirling beneath the town's serene facade.

Ella sighed, her thoughts drifting back to the day Michael had vanished. They had been exploring the outskirts of town, drawn by rumors of strange happenings near the abandoned mansion that loomed over Hawthorne Heights like a silent sentinel. It was a warm afternoon, the air thick with the scent of earth and wildflowers.

As they ventured deeper into the overgrown grounds of the mansion, a sense of unease had settled over the group. Shadows seemed to lengthen, and the breeze carried whispered voices that echoed through the crumbling walls.

Michael had been ahead, his curiosity driving him to investigate a peculiar symbol etched into the mansion's weathered door. Ella remembered the moment vividly—the creak of floorboards underfoot, the distant call of a raven, and then... silence. When she reached the doorway moments later, Michael was gone, as if swallowed by the shadows themselves. All that remained were his footprints in the dust and the faintest echo of his laughter lingering in the air.

They had searched frantically, calling his name into the echoing halls and scouring every corner of the mansion's sprawling interior. But there was no trace of him, no clue to explain his sudden disappearance. It was as if he had vanished into thin air, leaving behind only scattered clues and unanswered questions that haunted Ella's thoughts day and night.

"We need to find him," Ella murmured, breaking the uneasy silence that hung between them. Her voice was firm, betraying the flicker of fear that threatened to consume her. "We can't just sit here and wait."

Liam looked up from his notebook, his gaze meeting Ella's with a mix of purpose and concern. "We will find him, Ella," he said, his voice steady. "We just need to figure out where to start."

Jade nodded, her shoulders tense as she reached out, placing a reassuring hand on Ella's shoulder. "Whatever it takes," she whispered, her words a solemn promise.

Noah glanced down at the books in his arms, his expression thoughtful. "I might have found something," he said quietly, his voice carrying a hint of cautious optimism. "There are stories—old stories—that might explain what's happening."

As the group exchanged glances, a chill wind swept through the square, rustling the leaves of the ancient oak tree that stood at its center. Ella shivered, a sense of foreboding settling over her like a heavy cloak. Hawthorne Heights held secrets, and she was determined to uncover them—even if it meant facing the darkness that lurked within.

Noah adjusted his glasses, his expression thoughtful as he flipped through one of the dusty books he had brought from the library.

"There are old stories about Hawthorne Heights—legends, really. They talk about a cult that once thrived here, hidden in plain sight."

Liam leaned closer, his interest piqued. "A cult? What did they worship?"

Noah hesitated, his brow furrowing. "It's hard to say for sure," he admitted, scanning the pages for more details.

"But the stories speak of dark rituals, sacrifices made to appease some ancient entity. They believed it gave them power—power over the town itself."

Jade glanced uneasily at the mansion on the hill, its looming presence seeming to confirm Noah's words. "And you think this cult... they're still here? Still active?"

Noah shook his head, closing the book with a sigh. "I don't know," he confessed. "But something strange is happening in Hawthorne Heights. Michael's disappearance might be connected to these stories—maybe he stumbled upon something he shouldn't have."

Ella swallowed hard, her mind racing with possibilities. "If these stories are true," she said slowly, "then we need to find out more. We need to understand what we're dealing with."

Liam nodded in agreement. "Tomorrow, we'll delve deeper," he decided. "We'll search the mansion again, look for any clues that might lead us to the truth."

Jade spoke in a cautious yet optimistic tone. "We won't let fear stop us," she asserted, her voice unwavering despite the unsettling revelations.

As the sun sank below the horizon, casting long shadows across the square, the group stood in silence, each lost in thoughts about the troubling possibility of the truth behind Michael's disappearance.

They had stumbled upon something ancient and dangerous in Hawthorne Heights, something that demanded their attention and courage. "We'll uncover the secrets of this town," Noah declared, his voice firm. "Whatever it takes."

With one last look at the darkened mansion, the group dispersed, each absorbed in their thoughts and the weight of the revelations they carried. Tomorrow would bring new challenges and dangers, but also the potential for answers to unravel the mysteries shrouding their town.

Chapter 2

Shadows of the Past

Ella walked briskly down the cobblestone path that wound through Hawthorne Heights, her footsteps echoing softly in the evening silence. Beside her, Jade matched her pace, their homes nestled close to each other at the edge of town. The last light of dusk cast long shadows across their path, the fading sun painting the sky in hues of crimson and gold.

Silence hung heavily between them, each absorbed in their thoughts about Noah's unsettling discoveries. Ella glanced sideways at Jade, noting the furrow in her brow and the tightness around her eyes. They had been friends since childhood, their bond forged by shared adventures and now by the ominous mysteries that gripped Hawthorne Heights.

They had made a pact after Michael's disappearance—never to walk alone in Hawthorne Heights. The town's quiet streets had once felt safe and familiar, but now they seemed to whisper secrets that only darkness could reveal.

"Do you think Noah's onto something?" Ella finally broke the silence, her voice low but tinged with concern.

Jade sighed, her breath visible in the cooling air. "I don't know," she admitted, her gaze fixed ahead on the winding path.

"But something doesn't feel right. Michael wouldn't just... vanish like that." Ella nodded in agreement, her thoughts returning to the mansion on the hill and the dark stories Noah had uncovered.

"We need to be careful," she murmured, her words carried away by the gentle evening breeze. "If there's something dangerous in this town, we can't afford to underestimate it."

Jade's grip on her shoulder tightened briefly, a silent reassurance amidst their shared unease. "We'll figure this out," she said firmly, her voice carrying a hint of determination that sparked a flicker of hope in Ella's heart.

As they reached the familiar bend where their paths diverged, Ella turned to Jade with a small, grateful smile.

"Thanks for walking with me," she said sincerely, her gratitude tinged with the weight of their shared worries.

Jade returned the smile, her own expression reflecting a mix of concern and resolve. "Anytime," she replied, her voice steady despite the lingering uncertainty. "We're in this together, Ella."

With a final nod, Ella watched Jade disappear down the path toward her own home, the shadows swallowing her form as she walked. Turning toward her own house, Ella squared her shoulders and steeled herself for the challenges that lay ahead.

Tomorrow, they would delve deeper into the mysteries of Hawthorne Heights, seeking answers that might lead them to Michael and unravel the dark secrets that bound their town.

Ella walked up the steps to her porch, the wooden boards creaking softly beneath her feet. The familiar comfort of home greeted her as she unlocked the front door and stepped inside. The hallway was dimly lit, the soft glow of a lamp casting warm shadows on the walls.

"Ella, is that you?" called her mother's voice from the kitchen, the faint sound of dishes clinking in the background.

"Yeah, Mom," Ella replied, setting her bag down by the door. She could hear her mother's voice growing louder as she approached the kitchen, the aroma of dinner filling the air.

"How was your day, honey?" her mother asked, turning from the stove with a warm smile. "Did you and Jade have a good time?"

Ella nodded, though her thoughts were still weighed down by the day's events. "Yeah, it was okay," she said, trying to sound casual. "We're just worried about Michael."

Her mother's expression softened, concern etching lines on her face. "I know, sweetheart," she said gently, placing a hand on Ella's shoulder. "We all are."

Just then, the phone rang in the living room, its shrill tone cutting through the quiet evening. Ella's mother exchanged a quick glance with her daughter before hurrying to answer it.

"Hello?" she answered, her voice slightly tense with anticipation.

Ella stood in the kitchen, listening to her mother's side of the conversation as she stirred something on the stove. The words were muffled, but Ella caught snippets—questions about Michael, reassurances, and murmurs of concern.

After a few minutes, her mother returned to the kitchen, her expression troubled.

"That was Jade's mom," she explained quietly, leaning against the counter.

"They're worried too, Ella." "We'll find him," Ella said quietly.

Her mother nodded, her eyes reflecting both worry and pride in her daughter's determination.

"I know you will," she said softly, reaching out to give Ella a comforting hug.

"We're searching for him with the police. Everyone is doing their best."

As they stood in the kitchen, the evening shadows lengthened outside the windows, casting a quiet veil over Hawthorne Heights and its secrets. Ella held onto her mother's embrace, drawing strength from her support and steeling herself for the challenges that lay ahead.

Just then, the front door opened, and Ella's dad walked in, his expression tired but determined.

"Ella," he greeted warmly, crossing the room to embrace his daughter.

"Hey, hon," he said to Ella's mom, kissing her on the cheek. "Any news?" Ella looked up at her father, a mix of relief and worry flooding her heart.

"Not yet," she said quietly. "But we're not giving up." Her dad, James, a detective, nodded, his gaze meeting hers with unwavering support.

"We'll find him," he said firmly, his voice tinged with the weight of his commitment to the case. "And I'm starving," he added with a tired smile, his voice lighter as he tried to lighten the mood. "I haven't had a chance to eat all day. Is that my favorite meal I smell?"

Ella's mom smiled warmly, her concern momentarily easing as she nodded. "Yes, I thought it might lift your spirits," she replied, motioning toward the table where dinner was nearly ready.

"Why don't you sit down? I'll get everything set." With a grateful nod, Ella's dad sank into a chair at the table, exhaustion evident in his posture.

Ella and her mom exchanged a glance, silently sharing their worries about her dad, knowing that he would work this case tirelessly until he found a resolution. Despite the uncertainty that lay ahead, they were going to support each other through these challenging times.

They all sat around the table, the aroma of Ella's dad's favorite meal—spaghetti Bolognese, with a hint of basil and garlic—wafting through the air. The room was filled with a tense silence, each lost in their own thoughts, until Ella's father's phone rang, breaking the stillness.

Ella's dad glanced at the caller ID and immediately answered. "This is Detective Collins," he said, his voice alert and professional despite his weariness.

Ella and her mom exchanged a look of anticipation, their hearts racing with hope and fear. As he listened to the voice on the other end, Ella's dad's expression shifted, his brow furrowing in concentration. "I'm on my way," he said finally, his voice tinged with urgency. He hung up the phone and looked at Ella and her mom.

"They found something," he said, his tone conveying both relief and tension. "I need to go. Stay here, both of you. I'll call as soon as I know more."

With that, he rushed out of the house, leaving Ella and her mom sitting at the table, their minds racing with questions and hopes for Michael's safe return.

Chapter 3

Into the Night Detective Collins Pursues the Unknown

Detective Collins stepped out onto the porch, the evening air crisp and tinged with the scent of impending rain. He paused for a moment, glancing back at the warm glow of the house behind him, where Ella and her mother waited anxiously. With a heavy sigh, he descended the steps, the weight of exhaustion settling deeper into his bones.

Michael had been a fixture in their lives—watching him grow up alongside Ella, knowing his parents well. The thought of Michael missing was unthinkable, a twist of fate that defied the logical world Detective Collins inhabited. Hawthorne Heights was known for its mysteries, its whispered tales of things unseen, but he was a detective who dealt in facts, not folklore.

As he climbed into his car, the engine hummed to life beneath his touch. The familiar routine of gearing up for a case pulled him back into focus. Chief Johnson hadn't divulged much over the phone, only the urgency of the situation. Detective Collins knew better than to press for details; in their line of work, sometimes it was best to arrive with a clear mind and let the scene speak for itself.

The drive to the station was a blur of streetlights and the occasional drizzle hitting the windshield. He passed a small coffee shop, its warm glow inviting, but he hesitated only momentarily. In urgent cases like these, every minute counted. Besides, the station coffee was notoriously bitter, but serviceable in desperate times.

Arriving at the station, Detective Collins parked and proceeded inside, the looming investigation pressing down on him. He passed through the bustling lobby, the energy of the night shift palpable in the air. Colleagues nodded in acknowledgment as he made his way to Chief Johnson's office, where he anticipated the briefing that awaited.

Detective Collins settled into the seat at the conference table, his mind racing with anticipation as Chief Johnson began the briefing. The atmosphere in the room was dense with tension, filled with both uncertainty and the unmistakable presence of FBI agents.

"We've received new information," Chief Johnson started, his voice measured. "Earlier today, a shoe was discovered near the outskirts of town. It's believed to belong to Michael."

Detective Collins felt a surge of irritation. "Was this confirmed by Michael's parents?" he asked, his tone clipped. In a small town like Hawthorne Heights, communication with the families involved was crucial, and he felt sidelined by the lack of consultation.

Chief Johnson nodded. "Yes, they confirmed it as Michael's," he said steadily. "The FBI has taken charge of this lead due to its potential importance." Detective Collins frowned, his frustration simmering beneath the surface. He had known Michael since he was a child and felt a personal connection to the case. However, he quickly reminded himself that emotions had no place in an investigation of this magnitude. If he allowed personal feelings to cloud his judgment, he risked being removed from the case entirely.

"I should have been informed," Detective Collins stated firmly, though his voice remained controlled. "And I should have been involved in this search. The

FBI's presence can be intimidating in a small community like ours."

Chief Johnson exchanged a glance with the FBI agents, acknowledging Detective Collins' concern. "We understand your position, Detective," he said diplomatically. "But the priority now is finding Michael. We need to work together on this."

Detective Collins nodded, reluctantly accepting the situation. "Understood," he replied, his mind already racing with plans to coordinate efforts with the FBI while maintaining a foothold in the investigation.

As the briefing continued, Detective Collins focused on the details of the new lead, pushing aside his personal frustrations to concentrate on the task at hand—bringing Michael home safe.

Chapter 4

Shadows of Guilt

Back home, Ella tossed and turned in her sleep, haunted by thoughts of Michael. She half-blamed herself, regretting the decision to go to the mansion despite her inner doubts. If only she had spoken up, maybe none of this would have happened.

"Ella, are you awake?" Her mother's gentle voice broke through the darkness of her thoughts.

"Yes, I can't sleep, Mom," Ella replied, her voice thick with tears. "This is my fault. I should have never agreed to go to the mansion."

Her mother sat down beside her, pulling her into a comforting embrace. "Ella, this is not your fault," she reassured, rubbing her back soothingly. "Something happened to Michael, and it's whoever took him that's to blame."

But Ella couldn't shake off the guilt. Like her father, James, she had a strong sense of justice, and the injustice of Michael's disappearance weighed heavily on her young shoulders.

As Ella's mother tried to console her, her phone buzzed with a text message. It was from James:

"They found a shoe. Please call Michael's mom, Lori, to make sure she's okay."

"Ella..." Her mother's voice caught with emotion. "They found his shoe." Tears welled up in Ella's eyes as she realized the gravity of the situation. Her mother stepped out to make the call, leaving Ella alone with her tumultuous thoughts.

Moments later, Ella overheard her mother's conversation as she spoke with Jade's mom. "Oh my goodness, they found his shoe," her mother cried softly into the phone. After a long silence, she continued, "Can Jade come over with Ella? James doesn't think our kids should be alone right now, just in case... I can't even say it."

Ella hugged her knees to her chest, feeling the weight of uncertainty and fear pressing down on her. She knew tonight would be a long and restless one, filled with questions and anxieties about Michael's fate.

Ella felt great relief when Jade walked into her room in pajamas. "Ella..." Jade's voice trembled with tears as they hugged tightly. After a moment, Jade broke the silence, her words trailing off with unspoken fear. "Ella... Do you really think something..."

Ella looked at Jade, her own eyes filled with uncertainty. "I really don't know, Jade," she replied softly.

Both girls felt overwhelmed by the developments of the day. Sleep seemed impossible under the weight of their worry. They decided to FaceTime Liam and Noah to see if they had also heard the latest news.

Noah answered first, still half-asleep and adjusting his glasses. "What's going on?" he asked groggily.

"We're waiting for Liam," Jade replied urgently. "Did you hear about Michael's shoe?"

Noah's sleepiness vanished instantly. "Wait... What happened?" he asked, suddenly alert.

As they filled Noah in on the discovery of Michael's shoe, Ella thought she heard a door close downstairs. Assuming it was her father returning from the police station, she didn't think much of it at first. But as their conversation continued, Ella couldn't shake the feeling that her father still wasn’t home. He would have come to check on them if he had returned. Ella knew her mother was already asleep—she had said her goodnights to the girls earlier. The unsettling quiet only deepened her unease.

"Um... I'm going to get a glass of water," Ella announced, trying not to alarm anyone. She attributed her heightened anxiety to the day's events and didn't want to cause unnecessary panic. Slowly descending the stairs, her heart pounded in her chest. Each step felt heavy as she gripped the railing for support.

Finally reaching the bottom of the stairs, Ella looked around but didn't see her father's shoes or coat. The front door was unlocked, which was unusual given the circumstances. She hesitated for a moment, then quickly locked the door, feeling a rush of relief at the familiar click of the lock. Just as she started to feel foolish for being so scared, something caught her eye—a note on the kitchen table.

It was odd because Ella had just cleaned the kitchen with her mother and knew there hadn't been a note there before. The paper looked old, and the letters were elegantly joined together in a style of calligraphy she had never seen before. Ella carefully read the note:

"The sacrifice happens in 5 days."

Sheer panic gripped Ella as she raced up the stairs, her mind racing with questions. What did that note mean? "The sacrifice happens in 5 days." Was it related to Michael's disappearance? And if so, what could it possibly mean? Her thoughts spiraled into a whirlwind of fear and confusion.

Breathless, Ella burst into her room where Jade and the others were still on FaceTime. "Guys, someone just left this on the counter," she exclaimed, holding up the note with trembling hands.

Jade's eyes widened as she read the ominous message. "What... Who would leave something like this?" Her voice trembled.

Noah leaned closer to the screen, his expression grave. "Do you think it's a threat?"

Liam, stared at the note, his brow furrowed in concern. "This is serious. We should figure out what it means."

Ella hesitated, looking at her friends through the screen. "I don't know if we should involve my dad," she said slowly, her voice uncertain. "He's already so stressed with the search for Michael."

Jade nodded in agreement. "Maybe we should try to figure this out ourselves first," she suggested. "We can't risk distracting your dad from finding Michael."

Noah and Liam exchanged a glance, silently agreeing with Jade's reasoning. "Let's keep this between us for now," Noah finally said, his tone serious. "But we need to stay vigilant and figure out what's going on."

Ella nodded, feeling a mixture of fear and determination. "Okay," she agreed reluctantly, setting the note down on her desk. "We'll figure this out together."

As they continued to discuss their next steps, Ella couldn't shake the feeling that they were entering into something much darker and more dangerous than they had imagined.

Chapter 5
Unraveling Secrets

The next morning, Ella woke up first, not sure when they had fallen asleep or even when they had ended the FaceTime call with Noah and Liam. She certainly did not feel rested. As she slowly got out of bed, not wanting to disturb Jade and thankful that Jade was finally asleep, she made her way downstairs.

She heard her mother on the phone. "James... Lori saw the note. Sacrifice, what does that even mean? ...Of course I'm not going to tell this to Ella... Of course, please, James, be safe." Ella, not wanting to worry her mother, decided at that moment to keep quiet about the note they had found last night.

"Good morning, Ella," her mother greeted her with a tired smile, her eyes red, most likely from crying. "Hey, Mom, how's Lori?"

“Not good, Ella,” her mother replied. After a short pause, she added, “Ella, please don’t go anywhere alone... I mean anywhere.”

“Of course, Mom, I won’t. I promise.” Ella replied, trying to sound reassuring. Wanting to break the tension, Ella’s mom said, “Alright, kiddo, let's make some pancakes.” “And bacon,” Ella added, managing a small smile.

Ella and her mom worked together in the kitchen, the familiar routine bringing a sense of normalcy despite the underlying tension. As they cooked, the comforting smells of breakfast filled the house, momentarily pushing away the worries that had settled in their hearts.

Jade soon joined them, rubbing her eyes and giving a small wave. “Morning,” she mumbled, her voice still thick with sleep. "Morning, Jade," Ella's mom replied warmly. "We're making pancakes and bacon. Would you like to help?"

"Sure," Jade said, trying to muster some enthusiasm. She moved to help set the table, her mind clearly still on the previous night's events.

As they sat down to eat, the three of them exchanged small talk, each trying to keep the mood light. But the note and Michael's disappearance hung over them like a dark cloud, impossible to ignore completely.

After breakfast, Jade and Ella retreated to Ella's room to discuss their next move. "We need to figure out what that note means," Ella said, her voice low. "We can't just sit around and wait."

Jade nodded in agreement. "But where do we start? The mansion?" Ella thought for a moment. "Maybe. Or maybe we should try to find out more about the old stories Noah mentioned. There has to be a connection."

"We can start by talking to some of the older residents in town," Jade suggested. "They might know more about the mansion and any old rituals or sacrifices." Ella agreed. "Let's go see Mrs. Thompson. She's lived here her whole life and knows all the town's history."

With a plan in place, the two girls gathered their things and prepared to head out. As they left the house, Ella's mother called after them, reminding them to stick together and be careful. "We will, Mom," Ella promised. "We'll be back soon."

As they walked towards Mrs. Thompson's house, the morning sun shining down on them, Ella couldn't shake the feeling that they were being watched. The note they had received felt more like a threat rather than a warning. The town was quiet and almost eerie, and the silence between Ella and Jade was heavy. "Jade... Do you feel like we are being watched?" Ella asked. "Yeah... I got that feeling too," Jade replied.

Clinging to each other, they quickened their steps and felt relief when they saw Mrs. Thompson's house. Today, the house felt dark; Ella had never noticed it being so before. They both looked at each other, and with a nod, Ella led the way to knock on the door. As they waited for someone to answer, they took in deep breaths. Suddenly, the door opened, and Mrs. Thompson stood there, her eyes gazing at them. "Well... I knew you would be coming sooner or later," she said.

Chapter 6

The Encounter

Mrs. Thompson's house had always been one of those places in Hawthorne Heights that every kid whispered about but never dared to investigate. The old woman was said to know more about the town's secrets than anyone, and her eyes seemed to hold the weight of years gone by. As Ella and Jade stepped over the threshold, they couldn't help but feel a shiver run down their spines.

"Come in, girls," Mrs. Thompson said, her voice a mix of warmth and something darker. "I've been expecting you."

The interior of the house was dimly lit, filled with the scent of lavender and something else—something old and musty. The walls were lined with bookshelves, crammed with volumes that looked ancient. Ella and Jade exchanged nervous glances but followed Mrs. Thompson into the living room, where a fire crackled in the fireplace despite the warm day outside.

"Sit," Mrs. Thompson gestured to a worn-out sofa. "I suppose you're here about the note." Ella swallowed hard, her eyes wide. "How do you know about the note?"

Mrs. Thompson smiled faintly, her eyes twinkling with an unsettling knowledge. "This town has a way of revealing its secrets to those who seek them. The note you found is just the beginning."

Jade, her voice trembling, asked, "What does it mean? The sacrifice in five days?"

Mrs. Thompson's expression grew somber, her face almost distorted, as if she was remembering something from the past. "There's an old legend in Hawthorne Heights, one that speaks of a ritual to appease the spirits that guard this town. Every thirty years, a sacrifice must be made to keep the peace. If it isn't, the town will face a reckoning." Ella felt a chill run through her. "But why Michael? Why now?"

"The spirits choose," Mrs. Thompson said simply. "And they've chosen Michael."

Ella shook her head, refusing to believe it. "There has to be a way to stop this. We can't just let Michael be taken."

Mrs. Thompson leaned forward, her gaze intense. "There was no way to save my friend 30 years ago... My suggestion is to leave, and never come back... Never come back." All of a sudden, Mrs. Thompson's face began to change before Ella and Jade's eyes. They were unsure what was happening as Mrs. Thompson spilled her tea over her light pink carpet. It didn't look like normal tea, but rather something greenish. Ella and Jade exchanged nods, then started to run out of Mrs. Thompson's house, with her screaming after them, "You cannot save your friend... He's gone, he's the sacrifice!"

Ella and Jade sprinted down the street, their hearts pounding in their chests. They didn't stop until they were far away from Mrs. Thompson's house, breathless and trembling with fear.

"What just happened?" Jade gasped, clutching her side. "Did you see her face?" Ella nodded, her mind racing. "And that tea... it wasn't normal. Do you think she's telling the truth about the sacrifice?" "I don't know," Jade replied, her voice shaky. "But we can't just leave Michael. We have to do something."

Ella took a deep breath, trying to steady her nerves. "We need to find out more about this ritual and the spirits she mentioned. There has to be a way to stop it." They decided to head to the library, hoping to find any information on the town's history and legends. As they walked, they couldn't shake the feeling that they were being watched. Every rustling leaf, every distant footstep, set their nerves on edge.

When they finally reached the library, they were greeted by the familiar, comforting scent of old books. They quickly made their way to the history section, pulling out dusty volumes and old newspapers. The librarian, Mrs. Clara Whitmore, walked in as they were looking through some old clippings and books.

"Hi, ladies," she said. Today, though, she looked different. Her narrow eyes almost felt piercing as she cleared her throat and narrowed them even more. She whispered, "You should not be going around town upsetting poor Mrs. Thompson."

Ella and Jade looked at each other, scared and confused. How would Mrs. Whitmore know this already? "You know, ladies, the neighbors said that you two left running like bats out of hell, and ten minutes later the ambulance was called to her house." Not sure what more to say, Ella and Jade were unsure how much Mrs. Whitmore knew about these old legends. "Ummmmm…. We were just asking her questions, we didn't mean to upset her," Jade stammered.

"I understand, but she's old. Leave that woman alone." The "alone" felt very definitive, and with that, she told Ella and Jade that the library was closing early and that they had twenty minutes.

Determined to make the most of their time, Ella and Jade quickly resumed their search. Jade found an old newspaper article titled "The Disappearance of Matthew Clarke" from thirty years ago.

Ella discovered an old leather-bound book that seemed to hold more detailed accounts of the town's history. Mrs. Whitmore lingered nearby, watching them intently. Her presence felt oppressive, and the girls exchanged wary glances.

"We need to find something useful before she kicks us out," Ella whispered. Jade nodded, flipping through the pages of the newspaper. "Look at this," she said, pointing to a passage. "It mentions a strange ritual and missing children."

Ella scanned the book she found, her fingers trembling as she turned the fragile pages. "This talks about a cycle of disappearances every thirty years," she said. "There's something about a sacrifice to appease the spirits."

Mrs. Whitmore suddenly appeared beside them, her eyes icy and unforgiving. "Time's up, girls. You need to leave now." Her words made it clear that she wanted them out immediately. Reluctantly, they closed the books and gathered their things. As they walked out of the library, Ella glanced back at Mrs. Whitmore, who was still watching them with that unnerving intensity.

"We need to find out more," Ella said as they stepped outside. "Something strange is going on, and we need to figure out what it is." Jade nodded. "But we need to be careful. I have a feeling we're being watched."

As they walked away from the library, the weight of the mystery pressed down on them. The pieces of the puzzle still didn't make sense, and they worried about how they would save Michael before the sacrifice in five days. They knew they had a long way to go to uncover the truth and save him.

As they walked out, Ella felt completely defeated, having found nothing concrete. However, a couple of blocks away, Jade surprised her by pulling an old leather-bound book from her bag. "Look what I have," Jade said with a smile, holding the book up for Ella to see.

"Jade!" Ella exclaimed, half excited and half anxious. "We can't trust Mrs. Whitmore. Clearly, she knows something. How did you manage to sneak that?"

Pride filled Ella as she admired Jade's nerve. Before Ella could say anything more, Jade continued, not waiting for a response. "Now we need to call Noah and Liam to compare notes…"

Ella reached for her phone to call Noah but noticed several missed calls and text messages from her mom and dad. "Ella, where are you?" her dad's texts read. "Stay away from Mrs. Thompson's house. What did you and Jade say to her? Mrs. Thompson died. There's a town curfew. Go home straight away. Why aren't you picking up your calls? Are you okay?"

Ella's panic was palpable, causing Jade to stop mid-sentence. "Ella, what's wrong?" "Jade… Mrs. Thompson died," Ella said, shock evident in her voice as they stared at each other. "We didn't do anything, we just asked her questions," Jade replied, her voice now tinged with panic. "My parents must be really worried too. They've been trying to reach me."

"In that case, we need to get home right now," Ella said urgently, her worry escalating. As they hurried towards Ella's house, they knew their parents would be waiting, likely with a flood of questions and concerns. As soon as Ella and Jade walked into Ella's house, their parents, along with Jade's parents, Thomas and Sarah, were waiting anxiously. Relief washed over their faces as they saw the girls.

"Where have you two been!" Sarah's voice was stern, with a hint of tremble. "I'm sorry, Mom, we were at the library and my phone died…" Jade trailed off.

Ella's father looked at her, unsure how to break the news. "Ella… Jade," James began, his voice grave, "there's been another development. Another person has gone missing."

Chapter 7

Shadows of Hawthorne

After James had briefed his family, he knew he would be more useful at the station. Frustrated by the unfolding events, he drove with a heavy heart. In fifteen years of police service, he had never investigated anything more than a minor break-in or petty theft. Now, one of his closest friend's children was missing, and Emily Carter had disappeared as well—the daughter of Daniel and Elizabeth Carter, who had passed away three years ago. James recalled how the community had come together to support Emily as she lived with relatives until her aunt could relocate from Chicago to take over the family home. Emily had recently returned from college under mysterious circumstances, leaving James wondering about her motives.

Arriving at the station, James scanned his badge and made his way to his desk. The usual hustle and bustle of the precinct seemed oddly muted under the gravity of the situation. He met up with colleagues who were already deep into the case, their faces etched with worry. Sitting at his desk, he checked his voicemails, hoping for any breakthrough. One voicemail from Dr. Valeri Blackwell, the coroner, stood out. Dr. Blackwell confirmed that Mrs. Thompson had likely died of a sudden heart attack, ruling out foul play. This news, while a relief in terms of clearing Ella from suspicion, left James conflicted about the ethical implications of the investigation given Ella's involvement.

He quickly texted his wife: "Hey hun – received an update from the coroner about Mrs. T. It was a heart attack. XO."

He knew she was with Sarah, preparing food for Michael's family, and likely wouldn't see the message right away. He was grateful for his wife's nurturing nature but couldn't shake the pang of guilt over their struggles to conceive more children.

As he was finishing his text, Chief Johnson walked over, bringing him back to the present. "Hey James," the Chief said, his tone serious. "Any updates on Emily Carter?" James looked up, his mind racing through the details. "I'm still waiting to hear back from IT on the CCTV footage. Do you know why Emily came back home?" Chief Johnson closed the breakroom door behind him, signaling that the conversation was about to become more in-depth. "James, I spoke with her aunt earlier," Chief Johnson began, "and she mentioned that Emily hadn't hinted at any plans to return home. She seemed settled in at school. Her sudden return is raising a lot of questions."

James nodded thoughtfully. "Last I heard from her, Cathy mentioned Emily was studying finance. She seemed focused on her future." The Chief handed James a tablet, showing CCTV footage of Emily receiving a note from someone in a black hoodie on Oakwood Avenue. "We're waiting on IT to enhance the image of the note," Chief Johnson explained. "A note," James murmured, more to himself than to anyone else. "Who did you give it to? Harper?" Harper was known for his expertise in IT and decryption. "Yes, Harper's back from vacation early to help out," Chief Johnson confirmed.

As they delved deeper into Emily's disappearance, they noted the responsible nature of her character and the peculiar circumstances surrounding her case. There had been no activity on her credit cards, and her phone was left behind in her dorm—behavior that was entirely out of character for someone her age. The missing pieces of the puzzle only added to the growing sense of urgency.

James leaned back in his chair, a grim determination settling over him. "We need to find out what was in that note and why Emily returned home. Something's not adding up." The clock was ticking, and he was determined to find the answers before it was too late.

Chapter 8

Home Front Tensions

Ella sat at the kitchen table, her hands wrapped around a warm mug of tea that her mother, had made for her. The tension in the room was thick, almost palpable. Catherine moved around the kitchen, preparing dinner, her movements brisk and purposeful, a stark contrast to the turmoil she felt inside.

"Ella, you haven't touched your tea," Ella's mother said, her voice gentle but strained. Ella looked up, her eyes meeting her mother's. "I'm just… I can't stop thinking about everything, Mom. Michael, Mrs. Thompson, and now Emily…"

Ella's mother sighed, setting down the knife she was using to chop vegetables. She walked over to Ella and placed a comforting hand on her shoulder. "I know, sweetheart. It's a lot to take in. But you need to stay strong. We all do."

Just then, the front door creaked open, and Jade walked in, looking just as frazzled as Ella felt. She gave a small, forced smile and joined them at the table. "Hey," Jade said, her voice barely above a whisper.

"Hey," Ella said, reaching out to squeeze her friend's hand. Her mother returned to her cooking, giving the girls some space. "Jade, would you like some tea or something to eat?"

Jade shook her head. "No, thank you, Mrs. Harper. I'm okay. Actually, my mom wants to speak with you outside." Ella's mother nodded and stepped outside.

As James was leaving for the station, Thomas called to say he would be out of town, which left Sarah feeling quite anxious about being alone in the house. After discussing the situation with Sarah, Catherine agreed that she and Jade would stay with the Harpers until Thomas returned. "It's okay, Sarah. I'd be happy for you and Jade to stay with us," Catherine reassured her. Ella and Jade were relieved and happy to be staying together for a while, finding comfort in the support of their families.

As Catherine and Sarah came back inside, Catherine continued with dinner. "Well, might as well add more chicken for supper tonight," Catherine smiled, trying to alleviate the gravity of the situation, but the room grew quieter. Finally, Ella broke the silence. "Mom, we need to know more," Ella said urgently, her voice laced with frustration. "We have to understand what's happening. It can't just be a coincidence that both Michael and Emily have disappeared."

Catherine turned to face them, her eyes filled with worry. "I agree, Ella. But you both need to promise me that you won't do anything reckless. Leave the investigating to your father and the police. They're trained for this."

"But Mom—" Ella started to protest, but Catherine held up a hand to stop her. "No buts, Ella. I mean it. Promise me." Ella exchanged a glance with Jade, who nodded slightly. "Okay, Mom. We promise."

Catherine's expression softened slightly. "Good. Now, let's try to eat something. We need to keep our strength up." As they sat down to eat, the atmosphere in the house remained tense. The unanswered questions hung over them like a dark cloud, but at least they were together. And for now, that would have to be enough.

After dinner, as they cleared the table, Catherine pulled Ella aside. "I want you to stay close, Ella. No wandering off, even during the day. And always keep your phone with you." Ella nodded. "I will, Mom. I promise."

Catherine hugged her tightly, and Ella could feel the fear and love in her mother's embrace. "We'll get through this, Ella. We have to."

As Ella and Jade went to Ella's room, they decided that they indeed would be looking into this. They contacted Noah. "Hi Noah – any plans tonight?" Ella asked. Noah cleared his throat. "Hi ladies," he always addressed both Ella and Jade. "I don't have plans tonight. The police placed a curfew for 9:00 pm… was that a trick question?"

"Noah, listen," Ella said, her voice urgent. "Now two people are missing. We need to find out what's really going on. The police are doing their job, but they're not considering the supernatural aspect of this situation. We have to look into it further ourselves." Noah paused, processing her words. "Okay… but how do you expect us to do that?"

As they brainstormed their plan, the group decided they would tell their parents they were planning to visit each other's houses for the evening. The idea was to use their parents' belief that they were having a typical sleepover as a cover, allowing them the freedom to investigate further without arousing suspicion. They planned to go to Mrs. Thompson's house, even though she had passed away. They believed that she might have known more than she had revealed and hoped to find clues that could shed light on the situation. With the plan in motion,

Ella grabbed a bag and put their book from the library inside, along with an extra battery pack. She knew they might be out for a while, and with their phones being their main source of communication and navigation, having an extra battery pack could be crucial.

As they went downstairs, Catherine and Sarah were sitting on the couch, each with a glass of wine and a somber look. "Where are you two off to?" Sarah asked. "Mom, we are going to Noah's house to meet up with him," Ella replied. Catherine confirmed, "You two need to be in the house by 9:00 pm. There's a town curfew." With that, Ella and Jade walked out, saying, "We will!"

The evening was just beginning, and the eerie silence of the town seemed to follow them as they made their way to meet Noah and continue their quest for answers. As they made their way to the town square where they had agreed to meet, both Liam and Noah were already waiting for them. "Ok, let's do this," Noah said with determination. "We have to use our time wisely, guys. We only have about two hours until curfew."

The group had a detailed discussion about whether they should split up or stay together. Each option had its merits and risks. After carefully weighing the pros and cons, they ultimately decided on a plan that would maximize their chances of finding clues.

Noah and Liam agreed to head back to the mansion where Michael had disappeared, believing that the site of his last known whereabouts might still hold important clues. They planned to search the area thoroughly, looking for anything that might have been overlooked during the initial investigation.

Meanwhile, Ella and Jade decided to revisit Mrs. Thompson's house, they reasoned that her home might still contain valuable information. They hoped to uncover any hidden clues or personal items that could provide insights into her knowledge or involvement. The plan was set: Noah and Liam would explore the mansion, while Ella and Jade would investigate the house. This division of tasks would allow them to cover more ground and hopefully piece together the information they needed. As they parted, they promised to text each other when they arrived at their destinations and again when they left. Under no circumstances was anyone to separate. They all agreed and left.

Ella and Jade walked toward Mrs. Thompson's house arm in arm, the air feeling cooler as they went. "Ella…do you think this is a good idea?" Jade asked, her voice trembling. Ella squeezed Jade's arm. "We're all scared…but we have to do something."

With that, it was a silent agreement that even though this might not be a great idea, something had to be done. As they arrived at Mrs. Thompson's house, they first checked the door. Jade, hoping it was locked, was shocked to find it slightly ajar. "Umm, Ella, I think we're not the only ones who've been here…"

As they quietly and slowly walked into the house, they saw that everything was disheveled. Papers were everywhere, and the place had been completely ransacked. A once tidy house was now a complete mess. "What in the world happened in here?" Ella said wide-eyed to Jade. They started to make their way deeper into the house, seeing papers everywhere, most resembling bills or invoices. "Okay, let's get busy," Jade said.

As Ella and Jade started to rummage through files and books, they received a text from Liam:

"We're in the mansion—text you when we're leaving." Ella, feeling almost guilty for not being with the boys and worried about their safety, said to Jade, "The boys made it to the mansion. Just as Ella finished her sentence, Jade said, "Ella, I think I found something here." Jade picked up an old leather-bound book, covered in dust, with a complex design of shapes and intertwined lines on the cover. Ella and Jade looked at each other, not knowing what the book was but agreeing that it was definitely something they should bring with them for further investigation. Noah was good at deciphering these types of symbols, and surely he could help them.

As Ella and Jade continued their search, they came across a locked door leading to the basement. "Odd, who locks basement doors?" Ella remarked, scanning the area for a key. Spotting one hanging nearby, she grabbed it. "This must be it," she said, inserting the key into the lock. With a click, the door swung open, revealing a dark and unfinished basement. "Ella…I really don't know about this," Jade hesitated.

"It's okay, Jade. Put that chair next to the door to keep it open. We'll be quick," Ella reassured her. Jade complied, and together they descended the stairs cautiously, on high alert for any potential danger. As they reached the bottom step, they noticed a black circle on the floor, adorned with the same type of symbols as those on the book they had found earlier.

Ella took out her phone. "I've got to take a picture of this to show Noah," she said. Ensuring her flash was on for better visibility in the dark basement, she snapped a photo. In the instant the flash illuminated the room, they saw two alarming things: a dark shadow rushing towards them and a patch of blood on the floor. "Ella, watch out!" Jade screamed, fear gripping her.

Reacting swiftly, Ella shouted, "Jade, upstairs!" They sprinted back towards the stairs, but as they reached the top, they realized the chair blocking the door had been moved. Panic surged as the door began to close with alarming speed. Jade threw herself forward, managing to wedge her body through the narrowing gap, the door slamming hard against her. "Argh!" Jade cried out in pain.

Ella, right behind her, pulled Jade up urgently. "Jade, get up! We need to go now!" As they burst through the door, they collided with Detective Harper, Ella's father, who had arrived unexpectedly. "Dad!" Ella exclaimed, breathless and terrified.

Chapter 9

Shadows in the Mansion

Noah and Liam arrived at the old mansion on Willowbrook Street, its looming structure casting eerie shadows in the dimming twilight. The mansion, abandoned for years, had an air of mystery that both intrigued and unnerved them. Its once-grand facade was now draped in ivy, with broken windows and a front door that creaked ominously as they pushed it open.

"Are you sure about this?" Liam asked, his voice a whisper. "We have to find out what happened to Michael," Noah replied, his tone resolute. "Besides, Ella and Jade are counting on us."

The inside of the mansion was even more foreboding than the exterior. Dust-covered furniture, cobwebs, and an unsettling silence greeted them as they stepped inside. The air was thick with the smell of decay and mildew.

Noah pulled out his flashlight, the beam cutting through the darkness. "Let's start in the study," he suggested. "It's where Michael was last seen." As they made their way through the grand hallway, the floorboards creaked under their feet, each step echoing in the vast emptiness. They reached the study, a large room lined with bookshelves filled with decaying books. Papers were strewn across a massive oak desk in the center of the room.

Liam began rifling through the papers while Noah inspected the bookshelves. "Anything?" Liam asked, glancing up from a pile of old letters. "Not yet," Noah replied, pulling out a particularly old book. “This is the ancient Sigil symbol,” Noah said, holding the book to show Liam. “A what symbol?” Liam asked, a confused look on his face.

“A sigil book is a sort of grimoire,” Noah continued, holding the book and examining it, completely focused on each brittle page. “Legends say that it contains magic and is believed to hold mystical powers.” As Noah opened the book, a photograph slipped out and fluttered to the floor. He picked it up, his eyes widening as he recognized Michael in the photo, standing next to a group of people in strange, archaic clothing.

"Look at this," Noah said, showing the photo to Liam. "Is that...Michael?" Liam asked, bewildered. I "Yeah, but who are these other people? And what's with the old-fashioned clothes?" Noah wondered aloud.

"This looks like Emily Carter… And look at this picture, that looks like Mrs. Thompson when she was younger," Liam added.

Just then, a loud thud echoed from upstairs, making them both jump. They exchanged nervous glances. "Should we check it out?" Liam asked, his voice trembling slightly. "We have to," Noah replied, steeling himself. They cautiously made their way up the grand staircase, the wood creaking ominously under their weight. At the top, they found a long corridor lined with closed doors. The sound had come from one of the rooms at the end of the hall.

Noah reached for the door handle, his heart pounding in his chest. As he pushed the door open, the flashlight beam revealed an old bedroom, untouched by time. In the center of the room was a large, ornate mirror. It reflected their apprehensive faces back at them, but there was something off about the reflection.

"Do you see that?" Liam asked, his voice barely above a whisper. Noah nodded, stepping closer to the mirror. The reflection showed not just the room, but shadowy figures moving in the background, figures that weren't there in reality. Suddenly, one of the shadows lunged towards them in the reflection, and the mirror shattered into a thousand pieces.

"Run!" Noah yelled, grabbing Liam's arm and pulling him out of the room. They raced down the hallway and back down the stairs, the sound of shattering glass and their own frantic footsteps filling the air. Bursting out of the mansion, they didn't stop running until they reached the safety of the street. Panting, they looked back at the mansion, its windows now dark and foreboding.

"What was that?" Liam gasped. "I don't know," Noah replied, "but we need to find out. I think I saw Michael in the mirror. We need to tell Ella and Jade about this." As they caught their breath, Noah pulled out his phone and sent a quick text to Ella:

"We found something at the mansion. Meet us as soon as you can. Be careful."

Noah and Liam hurried away from the mansion on Willowbrook Street, their hearts still pounding from the unsettling discoveries inside. They walked briskly through the quiet streets, the cool night air adding to their unease. As they approached the town square, a police car pulled up beside them, its headlights cutting through the darkness.

The officer rolled down the window, casting a scrutinizing gaze at the two boys. "Good evening, boys," the officer greeted them, his tone firm but not unkind. "What are you doing out here so late?" Noah exchanged a quick glance with Liam, his mind racing for an explanation. "Uh, we were... just exploring," Noah replied cautiously. "We didn't realize it was past curfew."

The officer raised an eyebrow, his expression skeptical. "Exploring, huh? Near the old mansion, you know that's where that kid went missing," the officer continued, his voice tinged with suspicion. Liam nodded, trying to appear casual despite the nerves gnawing at him. "Yeah, we heard some stories about it being haunted. Thought we'd check it out."

The officer's gaze hardened slightly. "Well, I appreciate your curiosity, but there's a town curfew in effect. It's not safe to be out here at this hour, especially near that place. You boys should head home." "We will, Officer," Noah assured him, his voice tinged with relief. "Sorry about that. We'll head back now."

The officer nodded, his eyes lingering on them for a moment longer before rolling up his window and driving off into the night. Noah and Liam continued on their way, their footsteps echoing in the quiet streets. "Close call," Liam muttered under his breath, glancing nervously over his shoulder. "Yeah," Noah agreed, his mind still reeling from their encounter in the mansion. "We need to figure out what's going on. And fast."

They quickened their pace, eager to reach Noah's house where they agreed to meet Ella and Jade. The weight of their discoveries hung heavy on their shoulders, the mysteries of the mansion and the strange mirror playing over and over in their minds.

As they approached Noah's front door, his parents were waiting for them, visibly worried and upset. "Guys, it's past 9! Where have you been?" Noah's mom exclaimed, her voice a mix of panic and anger. "We've been so worried." Noah and Liam exchanged uncomfortable glances, both knowing they were in for a lecture.

"Um, I'm really sorry, Mom and Dad," Noah began, trying to explain. "We were out exploring and just lost track of time... We're really sorry." Liam nodded in agreement, "Yes, we're really sorry..."

Noah's father, clearly not entirely convinced by their story, addressed Liam sternly. "Liam, call your parents to let them know you're here and that you'll be staying over tonight. With the town curfew, this applies to everyone, even adventurous kids." "Yes, sir," Liam replied nervously, pulling out his phone and stepping away to make the call.

Noah's parents sighed, visibly relieved that the boys were safe but still upset by their late-night escapade. "Do you know how worried we've been?" Noah's mom continued, her tone softening slightly but still stern. "You can't do this again, Noah." Noah nodded solemnly, feeling his mother's concern deeply "I know, Mom. I'm sorry." As Liam finished his call and rejoined them, Noah's parents ushered them inside, their expressions a mix of relief and admonishment.

"We need to talk," Noah's dad said firmly, leading them to the living room where a serious conversation awaited. Noah and Liam endured a long lecture from Noah's father, who emphasized the importance of responsibility and obeying rules, especially during uncertain times. They nodded earnestly, their minds still buzzing with the eerie events at the mansion and the mysteries they had uncovered. After what felt like an eternity of parental concern and lectures on safety, Noah's dad finally concluded, "Alright, boys. You need to get some rest now. We'll talk more about this tomorrow."

Noah and Liam exchanged a glance of relief as they headed upstairs to Noah's room. The weight of the evening's events hung heavy in the air between them, but there was also an unspoken purpose to uncover the truth.

In Noah's room, they flopped down on the bed and stared up at the ceiling, both lost in their thoughts. The dim light from Noah's bedside lamp cast long shadows around the room, adding to the lingering sense of unease.

"That mirror," Liam finally broke the silence, his voice barely above a whisper. "What do you think that was about?" Noah sighed, sitting up and leaning against the headboard. "I don't know, man. It was like... something out of a horror movie. The way those figures moved in the reflection... And did you see Michael? It looked like he was there."

Liam nodded, rubbing his temples as if trying to dispel the lingering images. "Yeah, and what was with those people in the old-fashioned clothes? And Emily...And Mrs. Thompson when she was younger..." Noah ran a hand through his hair, frustration evident in his voice. "It's like we stumbled onto something much bigger than we expected. Like a puzzle with missing pieces that we're just starting to uncover."

They fell silent again, both lost in their thoughts, until Liam spoke up, "We need to tell Ella and Jade about what we found. They might have uncovered something too." Noah checked his phone for any reply from Ella, but found nothing. "Strange," he muttered, considering the possibility that they had been caught by their parents as well. Noah nodded in agreement. "Definitely. Tomorrow, we'll meet up with them and compare notes. Maybe they found something that connects to what we saw."

Liam glanced at Noah, concern etched on his face. "Do you think we should involve the police? What if there's something dangerous going on?" Noah hesitated, considering their options. "I don't know. We should gather more evidence first. Let's see what Ella and Jade have to say. If things start getting too weird, then maybe we involve the police."

Liam nodded slowly, seeming to agree with Noah's cautious approach. "Okay. But we need to be careful. Whatever's going on, it's not just about the mansion or the mirror. There's something deeper here." Noah sighed, feeling the responsibility settling on his shoulders. "Yeah. We'll figure it out, Liam. Together."

As Noah reached out and retrieved the ancient book from his bag, surprising Liam. "I thought you dropped it!" Liam exclaimed. Noah grinned. "I went back and grabbed it when we were leaving the mansion, before the officer showed up." Liam took the book from Noah's hand, flipping through its pages with curiosity. "What's so special about this book?" he asked, scanning the unfamiliar text. "And what language is this anyway?"

Noah peered over Liam's shoulder. "It looks like Latin, or something similar. We might need to translate it to understand more." Liam nodded thoughtfully. "Well, there's always Google Translate," he suggested with a hint of humor, trying to lighten the tense atmosphere. Noah chuckled softly. "Yeah, let's hope it can make sense of this."

As they settled in for the night, their minds raced with questions and possibilities, each eager to uncover the secrets hidden within the ancient tome and the mysteries that surrounded them.

Chapter 10

Unraveling Threads

Ella and Jade stumbled to a halt as they collided with Detective Harper at the doorway of Mrs. Thompson's house. His eyes narrowed as he took in their panicked expressions and the disheveled state of the front door.

"Girls, what are you doing here?" Detective Harper's voice was firm, tinged with concern and authority.

Ella exchanged a quick glance with Jade, trying to gather her thoughts. "Dad, we... we were just..." She faltered, unsure how to explain their presence without revealing their unauthorized investigation. Before she could come up with a plausible response, Detective Harper's gaze sharpened. "You know there's a town curfew in effect. It's not safe to be out here at this hour. And what's going on with Mrs.

Thompson's house?" Jade stepped forward, her voice trembling slightly. "Sir, we were just... checking on things. We thought we saw something strange earlier, and... we were worried."

Detective Harper sighed, his expression softening slightly. "Girls, I understand you're concerned, but this is not how we handle things. You should have informed your parents or me."

Ella nodded, feeling a mix of guilt and frustration. "I'm sorry, Dad. We just... we wanted to help. With everything that's been happening..." Her father's stern expression softened further, understanding flickering in his eyes. "I know, Ella. But this is dangerous. We have protocols for a reason. Now, go home. It's late."

Relieved that they weren't being further reprimanded, Ella and Jade nodded in unison. "Yes, Dad," Ella replied quietly. Detective Harper watched them for a moment longer before stepping aside to let them pass. "And girls," he called after them as they hurried down the path, "don't let curiosity get the better of you again." “We won’t,” Jade promised, glancing back with apprehension.

As they walked back towards Ella's house, the weight of their near-encounter with danger settled heavily on their shoulders. The adrenaline rush from their escape was fading, leaving behind a sense of unease and unanswered questions. “I can't believe we almost got caught," Jade muttered, her voice barely above a whisper. Ella nodded, her thoughts racing. "We need to be more careful. Dad's right. This isn't a game."

Jade shot her a sideways glance. "But what about everything we've found? Mrs. Thompson's house was ransacked, and that basement... those symbols and that shadow..."

Ella shook her head, her mind still reeling from the basement encounter. "I don't know, Jade. But Dad's right about one thing—we can't do this alone. We need to tell Noah and Liam everything. They might have found something at the mansion too."

Jade hesitated, chewing her lip in thought. "Do you think they'll believe us?" "They have to," Ella replied, her voice firm. "We're in this together now."

By the time they reached Ella's house, the town was cloaked in silence, the streets empty. They slipped inside quietly, careful not to alarm their mothers, but found a note on the counter from Ella's mother and Jade's mother. It read: "We brought lasagna over to Lori's house and left some for you in the fridge. We'll be back later. Love, Mom." Ella and Jade both felt a great sense of relief that their mothers were not home.

In Ella's room, they settled on the floor, facing each other with a blend of resolve and unease. "We need to figure out what's going on," Jade said, echoing Ella's thoughts.

Ella nodded, pulling out her phone to text Noah and Liam. She quickly typed: "Noah, Jade and I made it back safely. Let's meet tomorrow. We have to compare notes. Did you find anything at the mansion?" Sending the message, she looked at Jade. "Sent. Now we wait for their reply."

Jade nodded in agreement, her expression serious. "And if things get too weird, like your dad said, we'll involve him and the police. But for now, let's focus on what we know and what we can find out." Ella sighed, feeling a sense of relief knowing their mothers were safe and they had some time to plan without immediate parental interference.

Ella glanced at her phone, waiting anxiously for Noah's reply. After a few tense moments, a notification chimed. "They found something," Ella said, relief flooding her voice as she read Noah's message aloud. "He says they found a similar book at the mansion. They must have uncovered something important too." Jade leaned in closer, her eyes narrowing with curiosity. "What else did he say?" "He didn't mention details," Ella replied, typing a quick response. "Ask if they saw anything unusual in the mansion, like symbols or strange occurrences." As they waited for Noah's reply, the room seemed to grow quieter, the outside world fading into the background as their focus narrowed on the unfolding mystery. "I wonder if Mrs. Thompson's death is connected to all of this," Jade mused, breaking the silence. "And the missing of Michael and Emily Carter too." Ella nodded, her mind racing with possibilities. "There's definitely a connection. We just need to piece it all together."

Another notification pinged on Ella's phone, signaling Noah's reply. "He says they found symbols and an old mirror that did something weird," she reported, excitement and apprehension mingling in her voice. "They saw figures moving in the mirror, like shadows." Jade's eyes widened, mirroring Ella's astonishment. "That's... eerie. Just like what we saw in the basement." "Yeah," Ella agreed, her voice barely above a whisper. "This is getting stranger by the minute."

Before they could delve deeper into their thoughts, there was a knock on Ella's bedroom door. Startled, they turned to see Ella's father, Detective Harper, standing in the doorway with a concerned expression. "Ella, Jade," he began, his voice gentle yet serious. "I know you two are worried about what's been happening. Can we talk?" Ella exchanged a quick glance with Jade, a mixture of surprise and apprehension flickering in her eyes.

"Sure, Dad," she replied, motioning for him to come in. "What's going on?"

Detective Harper stepped into the room, closing the door behind him. He took a deep breath before speaking. "I spoke with Mrs. Thompson's daughter, Jessica. She's deeply concerned about her mother's death, as you can imagine. She said Mrs. Thompson was in the best shape of her life. I need to know, did she seem different when you saw her? And did you find anything else after going back?"

Ella hesitated, unsure of how much to reveal. "Dad, we... we found Mrs. Thompson's house ransacked," she admitted, her voice wavering slightly. "And there were strange symbols in the basement. We were just trying to figure out if they meant something." Detective Harper's brow furrowed, concern deepening in his eyes. "Symbols? What kind of symbols? Where did you see this?"

Jade spoke up, her voice steady despite the tension in the room. "We saw this in the basement. They were like circles with markings inside. And there was a shadow... like something moving." Her father's expression darkened, his thoughts racing. "In the basement? That door is sealed closed. We currently have a team trying to open it. Are you sure you went in there?" Ella shook her head quickly. "Yes, Dad. There was a key nearby that opened the basement door."

Detective Harper sighed, running a hand through his hair. "Listen, girls. I understand you want to help. But this is serious. If you see anything else, or if you hear from Noah and Liam about what they found, let me know immediately. Don't take any risks."

"We will, Dad," Ella promised, her voice earnest. "We just want to find out what happened to Mrs. Thompson." Her father nodded, a mixture of pride and concern evident in his gaze. "I know you do. But the coroner said she died of a heart attack, nothing supernatural about that."

"I'll leave you two," Detective Harper said, turning towards the door. "And girls, remember what I said about involving me if things get too strange. Don't hesitate." With that, he left the room, leaving Ella and Jade in a contemplative silence."I guess we're not alone in this anymore," Jade remarked, breaking the quiet tension.

Ella nodded, her mind whirling with thoughts of their discoveries and her father's words. "Yeah. Let's keep Noah and Liam updated. We need to figure this out together." Jade agreed, her focus aligned with Ella's. "Definitely. We'll get to the bottom of this, no matter what." As the door clicked shut behind Detective Harper, Ella and Jade exchanged decided looks. "We can't let this go," Jade said, her voice firm. Ella nodded in agreement.

"Let's see what we can find out tonight. We might not get much sleep, but we need answers." They grabbed Ella's laptop and settled on her bed, the screen casting a soft glow in the dimly lit room. Ella opened a browser and began typing in the symbols they had seen in the basement, as well as any Latin words they were finding in the book they took from Mrs. Thompson, going back and forth between the book and Ella's laptop.

Jade tried to pronounce the words, "Ok…Try typing AB….OMNI….MALEFICIO," she said, mispronouncing the word, pointing the word to Ella from the book. "Well, based on this, that means 'From all Evil,'" Ella translated. They continued this cycle, trying to make sense of the book. Hours passed as they sifted through websites, forums, and digital archives. Each new piece of information seemed to lead to another question rather than an answer. The symbols appeared to be part of an ancient language used in various rituals, but their exact meaning remained elusive.

Jade yawned and stretched, rubbing her tired eyes. "I know we don't drink coffee, but this might be a good time to start. Ella nodded, her fingers still typing furiously. "I know, let's go and make some, and maybe we can mix it with hot chocolate. The caffeine and sugar rush might help."

With that, Ella and Jade made their way quietly downstairs. As Ella started the coffee, Jade made the hot chocolate. “Ohh, your mom made chocolate chip cookies!” Jade said, grabbing a plate and adding a few of those. Ella smiled at how comfortable Jade was in her home; it made them feel closer during this time. As their half-coffee, half-hot chocolate was done, they brought that along with a plate of Ella’s mom’s delicious chocolate chip cookies upstairs and continued their work. Finally, they stumbled upon a website dedicated to historical occult practices. As they scrolled through the page, a particular symbol caught their attention.

"That's it!" Jade exclaimed, pointing to the screen. "That's one of the symbols we saw in the basement." Ella's eyes widened as she read the accompanying text. "It says here that this symbol is part of an ancient protection ritual. It was used to ward off evil spirits and dark forces." Jade frowned. "But why would Mrs. Thompson have that in her basement? Was she trying to protect herself from something?"

Ella shook her head, her mind racing. "I don't know, but it makes sense. Maybe she knew something or saw something that scared her." They continued to search, translating Latin phrases using online tools and cross-referencing them with historical texts. One phrase stood out: "Custodiam anima," which translated to "Guard the soul." "What does that mean?" Jade wondered aloud. Ella thought for a moment. "It could be part of the protection ritual. Maybe Mrs. Thompson was trying to guard her soul from something." The room grew quieter as they absorbed the implications of their findings. Ella's phone buzzed, breaking the silence. It was a message from Noah: "Found anything new? We're pulling an all-nighter." Ella quickly typed a response: "Yes. Symbols are part of a protection ritual. Mrs. Thompson might have been trying to guard herself from something."

As they waited for Noah's reply, Jade looked at Ella with concern. "We need to be careful, Ella. If Mrs. Thompson was scared enough to perform a protection ritual, we might be in over our heads." Ella nodded. "I know. But we have to keep going. We need to understand what we're dealing with." Noah's reply came through: "Got it. We'll look into it too. Stay safe." Ella put down her phone and turned to Jade. "Let's get some rest. We'll meet up with Noah and Liam tomorrow and figure out our next move." Jade agreed, and they both settled down, exhaustion finally catching up with them. As they drifted off to sleep, the symbols and Latin phrases swirled in their minds, hinting at the dark and mysterious forces at play.

Chapter 11

Unveiling the Gate to Truth

The first light of dawn filtered through Ella's bedroom window, casting a gentle glow over the room. Ella and Jade stirred awake, the events of the previous night still fresh in their minds. They had fallen asleep on the floor, the laptop and the book open between them. Ella blinked groggily, rubbing her eyes as she noticed the laptop screen still glowing softly.

"Jade, wake up," Ella whispered, nudging her friend gently. "Look at this." Jade groaned, stretching before sitting up. Her eyes widened as she saw the book open to a specific page and the laptop still on. "I thought we closed everything before we fell asleep," she murmured, her voice filled with confusion. Ella nodded, a sense of unease creeping over her. "I did too. But it looks like something, or someone, wanted us to see this." They both leaned in closer, examining the book and the laptop screen. The book was open to a page with an intricate symbol they hadn't noticed before, accompanied by a Latin phrase:

"Aperi portam ad veritatem," which translated to "Open the gate to truth."

"That's strange," Jade whispered. "Do you think this means something?" Ella nodded slowly. "It has to. Let's see what the laptop is showing." The laptop displayed a website they hadn't seen before. It detailed various rituals and incantations, including the one involving the symbol and phrase they had just discovered. "This is getting weirder by the minute," Jade said, her voice tinged with both fear and curiosity.

Ella's phone buzzed, startling both her and Jade. She picked it up and saw a message from Noah: "You awake? We might have found some new information about the mirror."

Ella quickly typed a response: "Yes. Book and laptop were open to a specific page when we woke up. Found a phrase: 'Open the gate to truth.' Might be important."

As they waited for Noah's reply, Ella and Jade continued to study the book and the website, trying to make sense of the new information. The room was filled with a tense silence, each girl lost in her thoughts. Noah's response came through: "That sounds important. Meet us at the library in an hour. We need to figure this out together."

Ella looked at Jade, determination in her eyes. "Let's get ready and meet the boys. We've got a lot to discuss." Jade nodded, and they quickly gathered their things, making sure to take the book and laptop with them. As they left Ella's house, the morning sun was already climbing higher in the sky, promising a new day filled with revelations and, hopefully, answers.

In the library, Noah and Liam were already waiting, their eyes shadowed with exhaustion but bright with curiosity. They had spread out their findings on a large table, including sketches of the symbols and notes on the mirror they had found.

"Morning," Noah greeted them, his voice tired but steady. "We found some pretty strange stuff. Take a look."

Ella and Jade added their discoveries to the table, discussing the mirrors and the shadows they had encountered. The four friends huddled together, comparing notes and sharing their theories as they pieced together the puzzle.

"The phrase we found, 'Open the gate to truth,' has to mean something," Ella said, pointing to the book. "Maybe it's a key to understanding the symbols and the mirror."

Liam nodded thoughtfully. "And if Mrs. Thompson was using these symbols for protection, there might be a reason she needed them." "Agreed," Noah said. "We need to dig deeper into this. The library has old records and books on local history and folklore. Maybe we'll find something useful."

The group split up, each taking a section of the library. Hours passed as they pored over dusty tomes and fragile documents, searching for any clues that could help them piece together the puzzle. Ella found a reference to an old legend about a hidden gate in the town, said to guard a powerful secret. She quickly called the others over to share her findings.

“Listen to this,” Ella said, her voice steady as she read aloud from the text. “The legend speaks of two mirrors—one representing light and the other darkness. These mirrors are said to control significant events and are hidden in places of great meaning, where light and shadow intersect.” Jade’s eyes widened. “That sounds like the mansion. There’s definitely something eerie and shadowy about that place.”

Liam nodded thoughtfully. "Or it could be Mrs. Thompson's basement. We know she had that strange, old mirror there. Maybe it's connected to the legend."

Noah's expression grew serious. "We need to decide our next move carefully. If Mrs. Thompson knew about these two mirrors—one good and one evil—it could be dangerous. We don't fully understand what we're dealing with yet." Ella's resolve was clear. "But we can't ignore it. Mrs. Thompson and possibly others were trying to protect themselves from something. If we want to understand what's going on, we need to find these mirrors." Jade glanced around nervously, her mind racing. "What if whatever is behind these mirrors is what took Michael and Emily? What if it's still a threat?"

Liam's voice was calm but concerned. "We won't know until we investigate further. But we should be cautious. We don't know what kind of powers or entities we're dealing with." Noah looked at each of them, worry etched on his face. "Let's head to Mrs. Thompson's house first. Maybe there's something there we missed, something that could give us more clues." They agreed and set off towards Mrs. Thompson's house, their footsteps echoing on the quiet streets. As they approached the familiar white picket fence and neatly trimmed hedges, a sense of unease settled over them.

"The front door is locked," Ella observed. "Maybe we can check around back," she suggested.

They made their way around to the backyard, scanning the area for any signs of disturbance or clues. Jade's sharp eyes caught sight of something unusual—a discolored piece of stone lying near the edge of the garden. "What's this?" Jade exclaimed, bending down to pick up the stone. It looked weathered and ancient, its surface marred with faint carvings. Ella joined her, peering closely at the stone. Recognition dawned on her face.

"This looks like something I've seen before... Jade, doesn't this resemble what we saw in Mrs. Thompson's basement?" Jade nodded slowly, her brow furrowed in concentration. "It does. This could be part of whatever she was using for protection." Noah and Liam gathered around, their interest piqued. "If this stone is connected to the mirrors and the legend, then Mrs. Thompson might have left us more clues," Liam mused. "We should take this with us," Noah suggested, carefully examining the stone. "It might lead us closer to understanding what we're dealing with." Ella nodded in agreement, tucking the stone safely into her bag. "Let's keep searching. There might be more." As they combed through the backyard, their eyes scanning for anything out of place, a faint rustling sound caught their attention. Turning towards the noise, they froze.

Standing at the edge of the garden, peering at them with wide eyes, was Mrs. Thompson's daughter, Jessica. "What are you all doing here?" Jessica demanded, her voice sharp with disbelief. She moved closer, eyeing them warily. "And why are you in my mother's backyard?" Ella stepped forward, trying to appear calm despite the tension in the air. "Jessica, we... we've been investigating," she began hesitantly, exchanging glances with Jade, Noah, and Liam, who stood silently behind her. Jessica's eyes narrowed, her gaze shifting from one face to another. "Investigating what, exactly?" she pressed, her tone skeptical yet tinged with concern.

Noah stepped in, his voice steady. "We believe there's something strange happening in town, something connected to your mother's death," he explained. "We found symbols in her basement and have been trying to understand what they mean." Jade added, "We're not trying to cause any trouble, Jessica. We just want to find out what happened to your mother."

Jessica's initial disbelief softened slightly, replaced by a flicker of uncertainty. "Symbols? What kind of symbols?" she asked, her curiosity piqued despite her lingering wariness. Ella took a deep breath, deciding to trust Jessica with the truth. "They were symbols related to two mirrors—one of light and one of darkness," she admitted, glancing at the others for support. "We think your mother might have been trying to protect herself from something." Jessica's expression shifted, a mix of surprise and sadness crossing her features. "I... I didn't know," she murmured, her voice barely above a whisper. She looked down, processing the information.

Noah stepped closer, his tone gentle. "Jessica, did your mother ever mention anything unusual happening, or anyone who might have wanted to harm her?" Jessica hesitated, her gaze distant as she recalled memories of her mother. "She... she was acting strangely before she died," she admitted reluctantly. "She kept talking about seeing things, shadows moving in the mirrors."

"That's what we found too," Liam chimed in, eager to validate their findings. "In the mansion and now in your mother's basement." Jessica's eyes widened, realization dawning. "You think whatever she saw... it caused her death?" Ella nodded solemnly. "We're trying to piece it together," she said quietly. "If there's anything you can tell us, any detail that might help..."

Jessica took a moment to collect herself, then nodded. "I... I'll help however I can," she promised, her voice steadier now. "My mother's passing... there's something more to this, I can feel it." Jessica nodded. "Let's start by looking inside the house again," she suggested, gesturing towards the back door. "There might be something we missed."

Ella, Jade, Noah, and Liam exchanged glances, their hope renewed. With Jessica's help, they were closer than ever to unraveling the mysteries surrounding Mrs. Thompson's death and hopeful they would also find clues leading to Michael and Emily.

Chapter 12

Unraveling the Mysteries

Inside Mrs. Thompson's house, the air was heavy with the residue of the recent police investigation. Yellow tape still marked off areas where the authorities had scrutinized for evidence of the break-in. Jessica led Ella, Jade, Noah, and Liam through the somber scene, each of them acutely aware of the gravity of the situation.

"The basement door is open now," Ella observed, pointing to the doorframe where the door had been removed from its hinges. "Last time Jade and I were here, we found symbols and even a small dot of dried blood on the floor." Cautiously, they descended into the basement, Jessica guiding them down the creaking stairs. As they reached the bottom, their eyes swept over the floor where the symbols had once been, but there was nothing left.

"The symbols... they're gone," Jade whispered, her brow furrowing in confusion. Ella retrieved her phone and pulled up the photo she had taken during their previous visit. "Look," she said, showing the group the image. "They were right here." Noah examined the photo closely, his expression grave. "I believe you, Ella. Something strange is definitely happening here." As they explored further into the basement, Jade's footsteps echoed softly on the concrete floor. She turned a corner and gasped, drawing the others' attention. "Guys, look at this," Jade called out, her voice reverberating in the cool, damp space.

They gathered around an old mirror with an ornate silver frame, tarnished with age. Noah reached out tentatively, running his fingers along the edge. "This mirror... it's similar to the one we found in the mansion," he observed, his voice low with apprehension. Liam nodded, his eyes narrowing thoughtfully. "But what's it doing here? And why does it feel like we're being drawn to these mirrors?"

Jessica glanced around nervously, her gaze lingering on the mirror. "I don't like this. There's something off about all of this." Ella nodded in agreement, her mind racing with possibilities. "Maybe these mirrors are more than just mirrors. They could be connected to whatever's going on in this town." Noah tapped his chin, deep in thought. "If the symbols and the mirror are linked, there might be a ritual or some kind of supernatural element at play."

Suddenly, a faint sound caught their attention—a soft whispering that seemed to emanate from the mirror's surface. They exchanged uneasy glances, the tension in the basement palpable. "We need to be careful," Jade urged, her voice tinged with fear. "These mirrors might hold the key to everything, but they could also be dangerous." With a collective nod, Noah placed the mirror gently on a nearby table and they started to back away. But before they could retreat completely, a dark shadow began to emerge from within the mirror, whispering, "We need to feed our souls..."

The shadow enveloped Noah, pulling him halfway into the mirror before the others could react. Ella, Jade, Liam, and Jessica scrambled to grab hold of Noah, struggling to pull him back.

"Noah!" Ella shouted, her voice filled with panic.

With a final, desperate yank, they managed to wrench Noah free from the mirror's grasp. They collapsed in a heap on the basement floor, panting and shaken. "We have to be more careful," Liam gasped, his hands trembling. "These mirrors are dangerous."

Noah lay on the ground, pale and shaken. "I... I saw something," he murmured, his voice barely audible. "It was like... another world in there." Jessica knelt beside him, her eyes filled with concern. "Noah, are you okay?" He nodded slowly, still in shock. "Yeah... just... not expecting that."

Ella helped Noah to his feet, her mind racing with the implications of what they had just witnessed. "We need to figure out how these mirrors work. There's more to them than meets the eye."

Jessica led the way back upstairs, her face pale but resolute. "We need to find out more about my mother's connection to these mirrors. Maybe there's something in her personal belongings that can give us a clue." The group moved through the house, searching for hidden notes or journals. They rummaged through drawers, scanned bookshelves, and carefully examined Mrs. Thompson's personal effects. Finally, Jade called out from the study, holding up a worn leather-bound journal.

"Look at this," Jade said, flipping through the pages. "It's a journal... and it's filled with notes on rituals and symbols." They gathered around Jade, peering at the intricate drawings and meticulous notes in the journal. Ella's eyes widened as she recognized some of the symbols from their previous encounters.

"This is it," Ella whispered. "This is what we need. Let's see if there's anything about the mirrors."

As they pored over the journal, they found references to mirrors being used as portals between worlds—gateways to other dimensions where spirits and entities could traverse. One entry, in particular, stood out: "The mirrors are both a window and a door. They must be handled with great caution, for they connect our world to the realm of souls. To control them, one must perform the ritual of binding, using symbols of protection and phrases of power."

"Ritual of binding," Noah repeated, his brow furrowed in concentration. "That must be what Mrs. Thompson was trying to do." Jessica nodded slowly, her expression sad. "My mother must have known about the danger these mirrors posed. She was trying to protect us." "Then we need to finish what she started," Liam said, his voice resolute. "We need to perform this ritual and close these portals."

The group continued reading, noting down the instructions for the ritual of binding. They needed specific symbols, phrases, and items to complete it—some of which were already familiar to them from their previous discoveries.

"We can do this," Ella said, her voice filled with newfound determination. "We have the journal, we know the symbols, and we have each other. Let's gather everything we need and perform this ritual."

As they prepared to leave Mrs. Thompson's house, Jessica hesitated, looking back at the living room where so many memories of her mother lingered. "Thank you," she said softly, her voice filled with gratitude. "For helping me understand what my mother was trying to do. I want to help, too."

Ella placed a reassuring hand on Jessica's shoulder. "We're in this together. We'll figure it out." The group left Mrs. Thompson's house, their spirits buoyed by a renewed sense of purpose. As they walked towards the town's library, their conversation shifted to the critical next step: entering the mirror to find Michael and Emily.

"We've gathered a lot of information," Noah said, breaking the silence. "But now we face an even greater challenge. One of us will need to go into the mirror." Jade's heart raced at the thought. "We don't know what's waiting on the other side. It could be dangerous." Ella, already feeling a sense of responsibility, spoke up. "We've come this far. If the mirrors are portals to another world, then we need to take that risk. We have to find them."

Liam nodded, his expression resolute. "This isn't something any of us can take lightly. We need to be prepared for whatever we might encounter."

Jessica's gaze remained fixed ahead, her voice steady despite the fear in her eyes. "My mother tried to protect us from whatever's in those mirrors. If one of us goes in, we need to make sure they have everything they need to stay safe."

As they reached the library, the group quickly began sifting through books and documents, searching for any additional information that might help prepare whoever would enter the mirror. The library, usually a place of quiet refuge, now felt charged with the weight of their daunting task.

The conversation soon turned to who would be the best candidate to enter the mirror. The decision was not made lightly. They needed someone both brave and knowledgeable about the supernatural elements they were dealing with. Each person's strengths and understanding were carefully weighed.

Ella, Noah, Jade, and Liam exchanged serious glances as they discussed their options. "It has to be someone who understands the symbols and the mirrors," Ella said thoughtfully. "But we also need to consider who can handle whatever is on the other side." Jessica, insisting it should be her because she was older, added, "I'm ready to take that risk." Noah, Jade, and Liam nodded, recognizing the complexity of the decision. They knew that whoever went into the mirror would face unknown dangers and wanted to ensure that the chosen person was fully prepared. With their plan in place, the group gathered the necessary supplies and information. As they prepared to leave for the mansion, Ella felt a mix of fear and determination. She had already decided that she would most likely sacrifice herself to save Michael and Emily but kept that decision to herself for now. The path ahead was fraught with danger, but they were united in their mission to find Michael and Emily and confront the dark forces lurking within the mirrors.

Chapter 12

Veil of Twilight

As they arrived at the mansion, the sun began its descent, painting the sky in hues of orange and pink, casting a serene glow over the ancient building. The group stood before the grand entrance, each carrying their equipment—books, journals, and the mirror they had retrieved from Mrs. Thompson's house. The mansion loomed ominously before them, its once-grand facade now draped in shadows as nightfall approached.

"Okay, let's start where Michael first disappeared," Ella said, her voice echoing in the quiet foyer. "That's likely where the mirror is."

They moved through the mansion, guided by their memories and the faint traces of Michael's last known location. The corridors were dimly lit, shadows dancing eerily along the walls as they advanced deeper into the heart of the mansion. Dust motes floated in the air, catching the dying light of the sunset that filtered through the windows.

"There," Liam pointed ahead, his voice hushed. "That's the room."

They entered cautiously, the air thick with anticipation and the weight of the unknown. In the center of the room stood an ornate mirror, its surface gleaming softly despite the fading light outside. It seemed to shimmer faintly, as if holding secrets within its depths.

"This is it," Noah murmured, stepping closer to examine the mirror. "We need to perform the ritual here." They set their belongings down carefully, arranging the necessary items around the mirror according to the instructions they had gathered. Symbols were drawn on the floor, candles were lit, and incense burned, filling the room with a faint, sweet fragrance. Ella took charge, her hands steady as she recited the phrases from Mrs. Thompson's journal, her voice infused with purpose. Each member of the group followed suit, their voices blending in a solemn chant that echoed through the mansion.

As they neared the end of the ritual, a chill swept through the room, causing the candles to flicker and the air to hum with energy. The mirror's surface rippled, reflecting distorted images of their faces and the symbols they had drawn. "We're almost there," Jade whispered, her eyes fixed on the mirror. Suddenly, a faint voice whispered through the room, barely audible yet unmistakably present. It seemed to echo from within the mirror itself, resonating with a mix of longing and sorrow.

"No," the voice pleaded softly. "Please don't close the portal. I need to find her..."

The group exchanged glances, unsure of what to make of the voice. But they continued the ritual, their resolve unshaken. With a final incantation, the symbols glowed brightly, casting a protective barrier around the mirror. The room grew still, the air clearing as if a heavy weight had been lifted. The mirror's surface settled, its shimmer fading until it resembled an ordinary glass pane once more.

"We did it," Noah breathed, relief evident in his voice.

Ella nodded, a sense of accomplishment washing over her. "Now we wait," she said quietly. "If this worked, the mirrors should no longer pose a threat. "Then, a faint, familiar voice echoed from the mirror. "I can't leave without her..."

"Michael?" Jade gasped, stepping closer to the mirror. Everyone turned to the mirror, their expressions a mix of shock and hope. "Michael, is that you?" Ella called out, her voice trembling. "I can't leave without Emily," Michael's voice echoed again, more clearly this time. "She needs me."

Ella's resolve hardened. "I'm going in," she declared, stepping toward the mirror.

"No, Ella!" Noah grabbed her arm, his eyes wide with fear. "It's too dangerous."

Even Jessica, the only adult present, tried to assert her authority. "Ella, you can't just— "

"I trust that you guys can bring us back with your mother's mirror, Jessica," Ella said firmly. "We needed a volunteer, and I'm going."

Taking a deep breath, Ella stepped into the mirror. The world around her blurred and then refocused, revealing a dark and eerie version of her hometown. She knew instantly she was no longer in Hawthorne Heights. It was as Noah had mentioned to her—a completely different universe, dark and ominous, as if trapped in perpetual twilight. The familiar streets and buildings were twisted and distorted, casting long, unnatural shadows across the ground. The air was heavy, filled with a strange, unsettling stillness.

"Michael!" Ella shouted, looking around the strange, distorted landscape.

Michael's voice called out, and soon he emerged from the shadows. At first, he smiled in relief, but his expression quickly turned to one of urgency. "Ella, what are you doing here?!"

"Michael, we have to go back. Your parents are worried sick," Ella said, glancing around nervously. "No! I can't leave," Michael insisted, shaking his head. "Emily is here. I saw her, Ella! She used to babysit me. I can't leave without her." Ella's heart ached at his words. "We'll find Emily, but we need to do it together. We can't stay here forever."

Michael looked torn, but eventually, he nodded. "Okay, let's find her."

As they ventured deeper into the shadowy place, it felt as though they were walking through an old town with dirt roads and ancient trees surrounding them. The place was eerily quiet, the only sounds being their footsteps and the occasional rustle of leaves in the cold, stagnant air. Ella was relieved to see Michael's face, feeling as though this moment would never happen, and yet, the unsettling atmosphere kept her on edge.

"Where did you last see her?" Ella asked, glancing around warily.

Michael looked around, trying to remember. "She was near those trees, and when I called out for her, she disappeared. I have no idea where she could be now." As they continued to walk around, a feeling of despair washed over them. The place was dark and foggy, as if the very air was thick with sorrow and fear.

"Michael, we have to stay focused," Ella said, trying to keep her voice steady. "We'll find her, I promise." They approached the area where Michael had last seen Emily. The atmosphere was heavy with a sense of foreboding, every creak and whisper making their hearts race.

"Emily!" Michael called out, his voice echoing through the empty space. "Emily, where are you?"

Ella joined in, her voice strong despite the fear gnawing at her insides. "Emily! Can you hear us?"

After what felt like an eternity, a faint, distant voice responded, filled with a mix of relief and fear. "Michael? Is that you?"

"Emily!" Michael shouted, his face lighting up with hope. "We're coming to get you!"

They followed the sound of her voice, navigating through the darkened alleys and shadowy corners of the twisted version of their town. The path seemed endless, twisting and turning as if the very landscape was trying to keep them apart.

As Ella and Michael ran faster and faster, it seemed that they could not quite get to Emily. As they ran, they felt spirits trying to hold them back—shadows of black and white that coasted through them.

"Don't let go!" Ella shouted, feeling the cold grip of the spirits tugging at her.

Michael clung to her hand, determination burning in his eyes. "I'm not letting go!"

They pushed forward, their resolve unwavering as they fought against the malevolent forces trying to separate them. The air grew colder, the shadows thicker, but they pressed on, driven by the hope of reuniting with Emily and escaping this twisted reality.

Finally, they burst through the last of the shadows and into a small clearing. Emily stood there, her face pale but her eyes filled with relief and disbelief.

"You found me," she whispered, tears streaming down her face.

Chapter 13

Fractured Reflections

As soon as Ella stepped into the mirror, the room fell into a stunned silence. Jade, Noah, Liam, and Jessica stared at the now still surface of the mirror, their minds struggling to process what had just happened. Jade was the first to break the silence, her voice trembling.

"What do we do now? It's almost curfew, and now not only is Michael still missing, but Ella's gone too!" Jessica, taking a deep breath to steady herself, reached for her phone. "

I'll call everyone's parents and let them know that you're all with me. They need to know you're safe and not to worry."

While Jessica made the calls, Noah began flipping through the pages of one of their books, his eyes scanning the text with urgency. "There has to be something here, something that can help us bring them back."

He paused, noticing a strange new crack on Mrs. Thompson's mirror, which had previously been flawless. "Guys, look at this," he said, pointing to the crack. Jade and Liam gathered around, their faces reflecting the same concern. Jade grabbed another book, her fingers quickly leafing through the pages. She finally stopped on a passage that seemed relevant.

"A crack means that because Ella went into the mirror, she created a disbalance, and the evil spirits are revolting," Jade read aloud. "It continues... 'Eventually, this mirror will be completely broken. Once that happens, they will be trapped in there forever.'"

"We need to find a way to fix this, and fast," Noah said, his voice firm. Jessica, having finished her calls, joined the group. "What did you find?" Noah explained the situation, showing her the crack and the passage in the book. Jessica's face paled as she took in the gravity of their predicament. "We have to get them out before the mirror breaks completely."

"There's a spell here," Noah said, pointing to a section in his book. "It says it's supposed to stabilize the mirror and bring people back from the other side." "Let's do it," Liam said, already grabbing the necessary materials. They quickly assembled the items needed for the spell: candles, chalk for drawing protective symbols, and an old, tattered piece of parchment inscribed with ancient runes. They arranged everything around the mirror, their movements hurried but precise.

"Okay, let's get started," Jessica said, taking a deep breath. "Noah, you read the incantation. Jade, Liam, and I will focus on maintaining the symbols."

Noah nodded, holding the parchment in his hands. He began to chant the words, his voice steady and clear despite the fear gnawing at him. The room seemed to respond to the incantation, the air growing colder and the crack on the mirror emitting a faint, ominous glow. As the chant continued, the symbols around the mirror started to glow as well, their light flickering like the flames of the candles. The mirror's surface shimmered, but the crack seemed to deepen.

"We need to keep going," Jessica urged, her voice strained. "Don't stop, Noah!" Noah's voice grew louder, more insistent, as he repeated the incantation. The mirror's surface began to ripple, as if trying to push against an invisible barrier.

Just as they reached the final words of the spell, a blinding flash of light erupted from the mirror, causing everyone to shield their eyes. When the light faded, they looked at the mirror, hope and fear mingling in their expressions. The crack had stopped growing, but it was still there, pulsing with an eerie glow. The room was silent, the air heavy with anticipation. "Did it work?" Jade whispered, her eyes fixed on the mirror.

They waited, their breaths held, hoping for a sign, any sign, that Ella and Michael were on their way back. But the mirror remained silent, its surface reflecting their anxious faces.

"We need to give it some time," Jessica said, trying to sound reassuring despite her own fears. "Let's keep watch and be ready for anything."

They settled in around the mirror, their eyes never leaving its surface, their hearts pounding with a mixture of hope and dread. Time seemed to stretch on endlessly as they waited, the fate of their friends hanging in the balance.

They all agreed that time was of the essence. Despite the cracks seeming to slow, the mirror's condition continued to deteriorate. They needed to find a way to communicate with Ella and Michael before it was too late.

"We need to somehow tell Ella that we don't have a lot of time," Noah said, his eyes never leaving the mirror. "Even though the cracks have slowed down, it's still getting worse."

Jade and Jessica were hunched over a book, frantically searching for any clue that might help. "Look here, Jade," Jessica said, pointing at a paragraph. "Maybe if we write them a message on a piece of paper, they could potentially get it?" Everyone agreed that it was worth a try. Noah grabbed a notebook and scribbled a quick, urgent note:

"Hurry up—the mirror is cracking. If it gets fully shattered, you'll be trapped there forever".

Liam took the note, folded it carefully, and approached the mirror. "Well, here goes nothing," he said, sliding the note against the mirror's surface. To their surprise, the paper seemed to be absorbed by the glass, disappearing from sight. The group watched, holding their breaths, hoping that their message would reach Ella in time.

Chapter 14

Race Against Time

Emily turned around, her face lighting up with a mixture of relief and confusion.

"Michael! I thought I was never going to see you again," she said, then her gaze shifted to Ella. "Where did you come from?"

Ella quickly explained how she had entered the mirror to save them. "We need to get out of here and back to the real world."

Emily looked skeptical. "How can you save us?" Before Ella could respond, a small piece of paper floated down, almost as if it were being carried by an unseen hand. It was so delicate that Ella wouldn't have noticed it if it hadn't brushed against her face. "What the heck?" Ella muttered, grabbing the wrinkled paper. "What is this?" She opened it and immediately recognized Liam's handwriting.

"Guys," Ella said in a half-panic voice, "no time to explain, but we need to go now."

Just as she finished speaking, they heard loud noises coming from afar, echoing through the darkened streets. "Oh no," Emily whispered, her face paling. "They're coming for me. A sacrifice is supposed to happen tonight, and I was picked first."

They all exchanged wide-eyed looks, the gravity of the situation sinking in. "Ella," Michael said in a somber tone, wiping away a tear that threatened to fall. "Once the sacrifice is done... Emily won't..."

They knew they had to escape right away. Determination replaced their fear as they formulated a plan. "Let's move," Ella said, taking charge. "We need to find a way back to the mirror. That's our only chance."

As they started running, the shadows seemed to grow thicker, the spirits around them growing more agitated. The oppressive atmosphere pressed down on them, but they pushed forward, driven by the urgency of their mission. "Stay close," Michael urged Emily, his grip on her hand tightening. Ella led the way, retracing their steps through the twisted version of their town. Every so often, she glanced at the note, Liam's words echoing in her mind. The mirror's cracks were a ticking clock, and they had to beat it. As they approached the spot where they had entered, the sounds of pursuit grew louder. The spirits were closing in, their whispers and wails becoming more distinct and threatening.

"There!" Ella pointed, spotting the faint shimmer of the mirror's surface in the dim light. They rushed towards it, their hearts pounding. The mirror stood as a fragile gateway between the worlds, its surface marred with the cracks that threatened to trap them forever.

"Go!" Ella urged, pushing Emily and Michael towards the mirror. Emily hesitated for a moment, fear flashing in her eyes. "What if it doesn't work?" "It will," Ella assured her, her voice firm. "We have to believe it will."

With a final, desperate push, Emily and Michael plunged into the mirror. Just as Ella was about to follow, something cold and strong grabbed her, pulling her back. She struggled, her fingers clawing at the air, but the grip tightened, dragging her away from the mirror's shimmering surface. "No!" Ella screamed, her voice echoing in the darkness. "Let me go!"

Her heart pounded in her chest as she fought against the unseen force. She could see Michael and Emily on the other side, their faces filled with horror and helplessness. Ella reached out, her fingertips barely brushing the surface of the mirror.

"Ella!" Michael shouted, his voice muffled and distorted through the barrier. "Fight it! Don't let it take you!" The grip tightened, and Ella felt herself being pulled further away from the mirror. Panic surged through her as she realized she was being dragged deeper into the dark world, away from her friends, away from safety.

Just as quickly, something appeared— not a shadow, but almost angelic. The image was large and white, and shiny, so bright that Ella had to look away from the light. It was blinding her. With Ella's eyes closed, she could not see what was happening. She heard cries and pleading, then suddenly a loud bang pierced her ears, followed by silence.

Thinking she must have died, Ella didn't want to open her eyes at all. But she heard a very familiar voice speaking to her. "Open your eyes, Ella." Ella knew that voice. It was a voice she had heard not long ago. Opening one eye at a time, she squinted at the figure. It was the brightest of white in shade and light. "...Mrs. Thompson...?" she said, still squinting.

"Yes, dear, it's me, and if you ever want to see your family and friends, you need to come with me now. The spirits will come back for you."

As Mrs. Mrs. Thompson, now reincarnated, stood before Ella with an almost ethereal presence. She looked much the same but noticeably younger, her attire a flowing white gown that sparkled so brightly it nearly hurt Ella's eyes. As Mrs. Thompson extended her hand, Ella was overwhelmed by a deep sense of peace. Despite the striking changes in her appearance, Ella felt an instinctive trust and reached out to take her hand.

"Mrs. Thompson, what are you doing here?" Ella asked, confused and so grateful to have been saved. "There's no time to explain… you need to go now."

Just as Ella was about to cross over, she hugged Mrs. Thompson and said, "Your daughter Jessica is with us. She really helped." Mrs. Thompson's eyes glistened. "I know. You have to go now." "But Mrs. Thompson, can you just say goodbye to Jessica?"

Ella pleaded. Mrs. Thompson handed Ella an envelope. "I don't know if this will make it, but if it does when you cross over, give this to Jessica." "I will," Ella promised, giving her another quick hug. Then, with one leg at a time, she crossed over, only to look back as the entire dimension began to crumble down. As soon as Ella emerged on the other side of the mirror, she was met with the anxious faces of Michael, Emily, and the rest of her friends. The oppressive atmosphere of the alternate world dissipated, replaced by the familiar surroundings of the mansion. The mirror behind her, now covered in a web of cracks, stood as a fragile barrier between the two worlds.

"Ella!" Michael exclaimed, relief flooding his voice as he pulled her into a tight hug. "We thought we lost you." "I'm okay," Ella reassured him, though her heart was still racing from the ordeal.

As they all hugged each other, Jessica was about to call the police to say that they had found Michael and Emily when Ella approached her. "Jessica..." Ella coughed, her voice still a bit shaky. "Your mother... well, she was the one that saved me." Ella continued, handing Jessica the envelope. "She said I was to give this to you." Jessica took the envelope, her hands trembling.

Her eyes filled with a mixture of hope and sorrow as she looked at the letter. She opened it slowly, her emotions surging. The words on the page were a comforting reminder of her mother's love and sacrifice. Jessica's mixed emotions were clear—relief, grief, and a profound sense of gratitude. She hugged the envelope to her chest, tears streaming down her face. "Thank you, Ella," Jessica managed to say, her voice choked with emotion. "Thank you for everything." Ella nodded, her own eyes misting up.

"We're all safe now. That's what matters." The group shared a moment of quiet, each reflecting on their harrowing journey and the strength that had brought them through.

As they prepared to leave the mansion and return to their normal lives, Ella, Michael, Emily, and their friends were acutely aware of the challenge ahead: explaining what had happened. The ordeal they had just endured was beyond anything that could be easily explained, and they knew their parents and the police would struggle to believe their story. The group exchanged glances, each one grappling with their experience.

"How are we going to explain this?" Michael asked, his voice tinged with worry. "They'll never believe us." Ella sighed, rubbing her temples as she tried to think of a solution. "We'll have to be careful. We can't just tell them everything. Maybe if we stick to the parts we can verify—like the missing people and the fact that we found Michael and Emily—they might listen. But the details of the mirror and the alternate world… that might be too much." Emily nodded in agreement. "And what about Mrs. Thompson? How do we explain her role in all of this?"

"We'll need to be honest but vague," Ella said. "We can say Mrs. Thompson helped us somehow, but we should focus on the facts we can prove—like the cracked mirror and the danger we faced. If we can show them some evidence, maybe they'll take us seriously." Jessica, still holding the envelope from her mother, looked up with a determined expression.

"My mother left a message for me. Maybe it can help us piece things together. But we should be prepared for them to doubt us."

The group nodded, understanding the gravity of their situation. They knew that, despite their best efforts, the true extent of their experience might never be fully understood by those outside their circle. They would have to navigate the skepticism and doubts of the adults in their lives while holding on to the truth of what they had faced together.

Chapter 15

The Forgotten Quest

Arriving back to town, it was like nothing had ever happened. The posters of Michael and Emily were gone. How did anybody know that Michael and Emily had been found? They had only just arrived. The town felt strangely normal, like nothing out of the ordinary had occurred. As Ella and her friends, along with Michael and Emily, approached the police station, it was eerily quiet.

"Hey, kiddo," said one cop. "Looking for your dad? He's in the break room," he said, smiling as if today was just a normal day. "Okay… thanks," said Ella.

They all looked at each other, confused. As Ella and her friends walked in, she called out, "Hey, Dad, we found Michael and Emily!" "Oh hey, kiddos… you found them? Were they missing?" he said, laughing as he sipped his coffee. "Dad," Ella said, growing more confused and frustrated. "Don't you remember Michael and Emily went missing?" Ella's dad looked at her with a bemused expression.

"I think you and your friends have been watching too many scary movies," he said, ruffling Ella's hair. As they were about to leave, he added, "If you're going home, tell Mom I'll be home for supper."

With that, the gang left, scratching their heads, completely bewildered. Outside the police station, they said goodbye to Jessica, who had decided to return to her mother's house to finalize things. Ella suggested, "Okay, let's go to your house, Michael. Surely your mother would remember if you were missing."

They agreed, noting that something strange was definitely happening. As they walked through the downtown cobblestone streets, Liam mentioned to Emily and Michael that their posters had been everywhere, and now there was nothing. They continued their walk and made it to Michael's house.

"Hi, Mom," Michael said, half-expecting his mother to come running to him. "Oh, hi, Michael. You're home!" she said in an everyday tone, not like he had been missing for days. As she hugged Michael, she spotted Emily. "Hello, Emily! I haven't seen you in years! What brings you here?" Shocked, Emily stammered, "Oh… I… umm… I missed home," half-smiling. "Well, I hope you stay for dinner," Michael's mother said warmly. The kids, nodding in shock and confusion, headed outside. It was as if none of it had ever happened.

As the gang agreed that this was all too strange, they decided it would be best for everyone to go home. Ella and Jade walked together in silence for what seemed like a long time. Finally, Jade broke the silence, "It's like this never happened," she said, more to herself than to Ella. "I know," Ella confirmed. When Jade arrived at her house, they hugged and said their goodbyes. Ella watched Jade go inside before starting to walk away.

"So strange…" Ella whispered to herself. As she continued her walk home, she noticed an envelope on the ground. At first, she didn't pay much attention to it, but something about it caught her eye and made her stop. It was Mrs. Thompson's handwriting, and it was addressed to her. Ella picked up the envelope, deciding to bring it home to read in a quiet space.

She hoped it might explain why everyone was behaving as if Michael and Emily's disappearance had never occurred. As she made her way home, she walked inside and called out, "Hi, Mom." "Hi, Ella," her mom responded from the kitchen, just as Ella had expected. "I saw Dad, and he said he'd be home for supper," Ella added. "Great, thanks," her mom replied, busy with dinner preparations. Without any further conversation, Ella told her mom she was going to her room.

Ella sat on the floor where she and Jade had recently tried to figure out what had happened to Michael and Emily. Now, as she sat there, the room felt different, the air thick with the weight of recent events. Taking a deep breath, she opened the envelope and began to read the letter.

Dear Ella,

If you're reading this, it means you made it safely and that my protection spell worked. You might be very confused because it may appear that no one remembers Michael or Emily being missing. This is because I cast a spell when you all returned that erased everyone's memory. They could never understand what happened, and we need to keep this a secret for your own protection.

You'll see in your bag the mirror—I had it placed there. I was not able to repair the crack, but I did make it stop. If you ever see the cracks growing, seek out Jessica. She'll know what to do.

Be safe—always.

With love,

Mrs. Thompson

As Ella reread the letter, she looked in her bag, and sure enough, the mirror was there with one crack. She traced the crack gently with her finger, feeling a mix of confusion and relief. No one would ever remember the pain they had all gone through with Michael and Emily missing. Although Ella couldn't help but feel elated because this also meant that the pain Michael's parents had gone through had also been erased, and she was happy for that.

Looking around her bedroom for a safe place to hide the mirror, she ultimately decided to place it on top of her closet, inside a box full of winter sweaters. Covered in her sweaters, she felt this was the safest place it could be. As she closed her closet, she fell onto her bed, still reeling from the series of events that had occurred… or now not occurred. She couldn't help but wonder if this would ever happen again. And with those thoughts, Ella realized that she hadn't slept well in what felt like a very long time. As this realization settled in, her eyes began to feel heavy, and for the first time in days, Ella fell into a deep sleep.

Chapter 16

Cracks in the Calm

Months had passed since the ordeal of Michael and Emily's disappearance. Emily had returned to college and continued her studies, keeping Michael updated on her progress. She often told him that her college, Westbridge University, was a great place and suggested he consider it at some point. Michael was also doing well, having returned to his old self, albeit a bit more cautious. School had started, and it really felt like things were returning to normal.

The gang had not been back to the mansion and had sworn never to return, saying that they would be tempting fate again. Ella and Jade's friendship was stronger than ever, and even though everyone had forgotten what had occurred, they had not forgotten how much they were there for each other during that time.

The cool air had settled in Hawthorne Heights, with the trees changing from their leafy greens to the beautiful foliage of oranges and reds. One day, Ella and Jade came home from school, noticing the change in the weather.

They were about to make their way to the café when Ella said, "I'm going to run home quickly and grab a sweater." Jade, all smiles, replied, "Sure, I'll tag along."

With that, the duo made their way to Ella's house, talking about their upcoming plans for a school science project. They walked inside the house, greeted Ella's parents, and made their way to Ella's room. As Ella looked for her sweater, she was reminded that it was in a box in her closet.

As she took the box out, Jade continued talking about the school science project. "I think we can…," Jade began, but Ella, half-listening, was sharply reminded that she had placed the mirror there months ago and hadn't thought about it since. Anxiously, she started removing the sweaters one by one, carefully.

"Ella… are you even listening to me?" Jade joked. Ella finally found the mirror and, carefully picking it up, she noticed something that made her face turn half scared and surprised. There were now two more cracks in the mirror. Ella's heart sank. She felt a wave of anxiety wash over her as she stared at the additional cracks. "Jade," she whispered, "we have a problem." Jade, noticing the change in Ella's demeanor, stopped talking and looked over.

"What is it?" Ella held up the mirror, showing Jade the new cracks. "There are more cracks. Mrs. Thompson said the cracks had stopped." Jade's eyes widened. "What does this mean?" Ella shook her head, feeling a chill run down her spine. "I don't know, but I think we need to talk to Jessica. She'll know what to do." Jade nodded, realizing the gravity of the situation. "Okay, let's go. We can't ignore this."

As Ella grabbed a sweater, she carefully put the mirror in her backpack. Jade, meanwhile, was texting Liam to give him a heads up on what was occurring and to wait at the café. Liam replied immediately, "This is not good. We need to contact Jessica ASAP."

Ella looked at Jade and said, "We'll call Jessica once we're out of the house." Jade nodded in agreement, and as soon as they walked outside, they attempted to call Jessica on her cell phone, but there was no answer. Ella decided to text her as well: "There are more cracks in the mirror. Call me back, please."

Ella and Jade continued their walk to the café, with Ella attempting to call Jessica two more times without success. They met up at the Cornerstone Café, where Liam, Noah, and Michael were anxiously waiting for them. Noah was the first to break the silence. "Here, ladies, I placed your order…. Now spill." Just as Ella was about to explain the situation, she received a text. Thinking it was from Jessica, Ella felt a brief sense of relief. But this was short-lived when she read the message: "Jessica is gone."

Ella's heart sank as she showed the text to the others. "What do we do now?" Jade asked, her voice trembling slightly. "We need to figure out who sent this message and what happened to Jessica," Michael said, his tone serious. "We can't let this go."

Acknowledgments

I want to extend my deepest gratitude to Melinda for her unwavering support and encouragement throughout the writing of this book. Your insightful feedback and constant encouragement have been invaluable in shaping this story. Your patience and dedication to reading through countless drafts made all the difference. Thank you for believing in me and helping bring this project to life.

I also want to express my deepest appreciation to my husband John, who has been my rock during this entire process. Your love, support, and belief in me have been the foundation that kept me going. Thank you for standing by my side and helping me achieve this dream.

www.ingramcontent.com/pod-product-compliance
Lightning Source LLC
Chambersburg PA
CBHW072031170626
46811CB00008B/3037

* 9 7 8 1 0 6 9 0 0 0 2 1 7 *